Supernatural

An Anthology of Magic and Secrets

By

Heather Beck

Treasure Cove Books

Published by
Treasure Cove Books

Library and Archives Canada Cataloguing in Publication

Beck, Heather, 1985-
          Supernatural : an anthology of magic and secrets/by Heather Beck.

Short stories.
ISBN 978-1-926990-18-7

          I. Title.

PS8603.E423S96 2013   jC813'.6   C2013-901413-6

Table Of Contents:

Black Magic Wish

"Today was amazing," Jamie Banks said happily, as she followed her parents into their house. "Thank you so much."

"It's your birthday and you deserve it," Mr. Banks replied, while affectionately stroking Jamie's hair.

"Yes," Mrs. Banks agreed. "Turning thirteen is a big deal."

"It doesn't seem like a big deal to me," Jamie said, more preoccupied with thoughts of her wonderful day.

Mr. and Mrs. Banks had taken Jamie to Wild Africa — a cool safari theme park where visitors could get close to a variety of animals. It also had a superb restaurant that served fancy meals and delicious desserts. What impressed Jamie even more than Wild Africa's many amazing features was her parent's decision to take her there. Admission to Wild Africa was very highly priced — something that always made the Banks uncomfortable whenever Jamie asked to go there. However, as a very special birthday present, they'd saved enough money and taken her to Wild Africa.

"Being a teenager is a *very* big deal!" Mrs. Banks cried, startling Jamie in the process.

"If you say so," Jamie muttered, watching as her father placed his hand on her mother's shoulder in a soothing manner.

"I didn't mean to shout," Mrs. Banks apologized.

"That's okay," Jamie replied, as she looked closely at her mother. For some reason, she looked nervous and worn out.

"You should go to bed, Jamie," Mr. Banks suggested. "After all, you have school tomorrow."

"Alright," Jamie said, before walking towards the staircase which led to her bedroom. "Goodnight."

After Jamie had exited the room, Mr. and Mrs. Banks stood silently. They looked at each other with worry in their eyes.

"Do you think we did the right thing?" Mrs. Banks asked, finally breaking the silence.

"Does it really matter what I think?" Mr. Banks replied. "We made the decision thirteen years ago. There's no going back now."

"Everything will be all right, won't it, Sam?" Mrs. Banks asked, as she grasped her husband tightly.

Mr. Bank's expression softened as he embraced his wife. "We were very young and naive when we made the decision to have Jamie blessed by Madeline. We also had no idea that Madeline was practicing black magic."

"You don't think there was anything bad in the blessing she bestowed upon Jamie, do you?"

"Everything will be fine," Mr. Banks comforted his wife.

As Mr. Banks held Mrs. Banks, he was grateful that she couldn't see his expression of doubt.

* * *

It was a late Monday morning as Jamie walked down the school hallway. She was heading to English class and was just about to open the classroom door when someone shouted to her.

"Jamie! Jamie! Jamie!"

Jamie stopped at the door and turned around to see her best friend, Stephanie, hurrying towards her.

"What's wrong?" Jamie asked in concern, not used to seeing her friend act so boisterous.

"Nothing's wrong," Stephanie replied, lowering her voice as she reached Jamie's side. "Everything is great – for you, anyway."

"What do you mean?" Jamie asked, while readjusting the backpack that was slung over her shoulder.

"I mean that you should be really happy!" Stephanie exclaimed.

"Why?" Jamie asked through a sigh, getting annoyed at her friend's ambiguity.

"Because..." Stephanie answered, pausing slightly for dramatic effect, "Craig is going to ask you to the school dance!"

Jamie couldn't stop her mouth from falling open. "How do you know this?" she demanded in an almost breathless tone.

"I was in the library when I heard Craig talking to his best friend, Martin. Craig said he was going to ask you to the dance. Neither of them knew I was there."

"Are you sure you heard correctly?" Jamie asked doubtfully. She knew that Stephanie would never lie to her, especially about something so important. After all, Jamie had been crushing on Craig, the school's most popular boy, for three years now. It just seemed very unlikely that he'd ask her to the dance since he could practically go with anyone he wanted.

"Yes," Stephanie reassured Jamie.

"Wow," Jamie muttered dreamily as she leaned against the door.

Suddenly, the door swung open. Jamie began to fall and would've landed on her backside if someone hadn't caught her from behind.

"The floor is no place for a lady," a male voice said in an amused tone.

Jamie wriggled out of the guy's grasp and then turned around to see that it was Richie, her long-time classmate, who'd caught her. "Be quiet," she snapped as her face reddened.

"Don't be embarrassed about falling into my arms," Richie replied with a mischievous smile.

"I would have rather fallen on the ground."

"Ouch!" Richie cried dramatically, while placing his hand over his heart. "Surely you don't mean that."

"Get real," Jamie said briskly as she stormed into the classroom. She felt a little bad about being rude to Richie, but did he really have to draw even more attention to her?

Stephanie followed Jamie into the class, but not before sharing a quick laugh with Richie. "Real smooth," Jamie heard Stephanie mutter to Richie before sitting down.

When Craig entered the classroom, Jamie immediately forgot about her embarrassing moment. Her heart raced as she cast Craig a friendly smile. She was delighted when he returned the gesture.

Although English was Jamie's favorite subject, she just couldn't concentrate. Instead, she stared longingly at Craig, noting his tall, athletic build, perfectly-combed blonde hair, sparkling blue eyes and that cute little cleft in his chin.

Finally the bell rang, signaling the end of class. Jamie took a long time gathering her books, hoping to give Craig a chance to talk to her.

"Hey, Jamie. How are you?" Craig greeted in a deep tone as he approached her desk. Martin lingered behind Craig, watching them carefully.

"I'm...I'm good," she stuttered. "How are you?"

"Great – as always."

Jamie smiled shyly. *He has such good self-esteem,* she thought with admiration.

"I wanted to ask you something," Craig began.

"What is it?" Jamie interrupted excitedly.

"It's about the dance. You'd like to go with me, right?"

"Of course!" Jamie replied quickly.

"Then it's a date," Craig said, smiling confidently.

In the background, Martin snickered. However, Jamie ignored him; she was way too smitten with Craig to even think about anyone else.

* * *

For the next few days, Jamie's mind was preoccupied with thoughts of Craig and the upcoming dance. Her happiness and excitement hadn't waned, although she was a bit disappointed that Craig hadn't really talked to her since asking her to the dance.

Jamie's anticipation made the days go by slowly. When the night of the school dance finally came, she was extremely excited. She could hardly even stand still as Mrs. Banks tried to fasten some beautiful silver jewelry around her neck.

"Hold still," Mrs. Banks instructed as Jamie tapped her foot impatiently.

"Sorry," Jamie muttered sheepishly.

"Nervous?" Mrs. Banks asked, as she finally clasped the necklace and then stepped back to admire her daughter's beauty.

"A little," Jamie admitted, while biting her lip.

"Don't do that," Mrs. Banks scolded gently. "You'll ruin your lipstick."

Jamie turned away from her mother to look at herself in the full-length mirror. She looked very pretty in a light blue dress and all that silver jewelry. Her hair was curled and a light blue barrette was placed above each ear to keep her golden curls from falling in front of her face.

"You look lovely," Mrs. Banks commented sincerely. "Craig is very lucky to have you as his date."

Jamie resisted the urge to inform her mother that *she* was the lucky one in having Craig as her date. Instead, she said, "I better go now – Dad will be waiting."

"Have a wonderful time, Jamie."

Jamie walked carefully down the stairs; she wasn't used to wearing high heels, and she prayed that she'd get through the night without falling flat on her face.

"You look very pretty," Mr. Banks commented when Jamie entered the car.

"So I've heard," Jamie replied with a smile, feeling more confident than ever before.

Although it wasn't a long drive to Jamie's school, she wished Craig would've somehow picked her up. She knew her parents would be impressed by him – who wouldn't be? Jamie couldn't deny that Craig's decision to meet her at the dance disappointed her. However, as she exited the family car and walked into the middle school's gym, her disappointment disappeared and was replaced with excitement.

The gym was beautifully decorated with red and white streamers. A large model of the school's mascot – an eagle in flight – was placed on the gym's stage. Some teenagers danced to the upbeat music, while others chatted loudly over the sound system.

Eagerly, Jamie searched the crowd. She couldn't wait to find Craig and officially begin their first date.

"Jamie!" someone called frantically.

Turning around, Jamie saw Stephanie. She was wearing a long, silky pink dress and carrying a fluffy pink handbag. She would've looked like a princess if it wasn't for the horrible expression upon her face.

"What's wrong?" Jamie asked in concern. She couldn't stop her mind from wandering to the last time she'd asked Stephanie that question. It was right before she received the wonderful news that Craig was going to ask her to the dance.

"Everything! We have to leave right now." Stephanie tried to pull Jamie towards the gym's exit, but she was met with resistance.

"I just got here," Jamie protested. "I can't leave – Craig will be waiting for me."

"He definitely wants to see you," Stephanie muttered angrily, "but not in the way you think he does."

"What do you mean?" Jamie demanded in confusion.

"Nothing. Let's go."

"Not until you tell me what's going on," Jamie insisted.

Jamie had hardly finished her sentence when a hand landed roughly on her shoulder. She let out a small gasp before turning around to face Martin.

7

"I've got date number ten!" Martin called out with a mocking laugh.

"Huh?" Jamie said in bewilderment.

"Come on," Martin insisted. "Craig is looking for you."

"Leave her alone, jerk," Stephanie snapped at Martin.

Utterly confused, Jamie allowed Martin to guide her towards Craig.

Stephanie said something in a desperate tone, but Jamie couldn't hear her amid all the commotion. There were nine girls standing around Craig. They all looked angry, and three of them were even yelling at him.

"Craig has ten dates," Martin announced to a group of boys who stood nearby. "You said he couldn't do it, but he did. Pay up, losers!"

Jamie looked on in horror as the four boys each handed ten dollars to Craig. All nine girls began yelling at a smug-looking Craig. Jamie was the only one who didn't speak.

How could he? Jamie thought as tears brimmed in her eyes. *How could he ask me out just to win a bet?*

As the other girls marched off angrily, Jamie was left standing with Craig and Martin. It took all of her strength and willpower to look at Craig in the eyes. "Do you have any feelings for me at all?" she hardly managed to choke out, while tears began rolling down her face.

Martin snorted, but Craig had enough decency to appear somewhat sheepish.

"This has nothing to do with you or any of the girls," Craig replied. "I just needed money for the new City Wars video game."

"How could you be so cruel?" Jamie tried to demand harshly. However, her quivering voice and tear-stained face prevented her from looking tough.

"It's a guy thing," Craig replied with a shrug.

"Yeah, you wouldn't understand," Martin chimed in.

With a stone-cold expression, Stephanie glared at Martin and Craig. "What you have done is not a guy thing – it's a jerk thing."

"It's actually an *I don't care* thing," Martin stated, before nudging Craig towards another part of the gym.

"You'll get suspended for this!" Stephanie called after the two boys.

"Nobody will tell the principal," Jamie stated flatly. "It's too embarrassing."

"Don't feel like that," Stephanie replied. "It's Craig, Martin, and those four boys who should be embarrassed – they're immature idiots."

As Jamie saw the sympathy and compassion in Stephanie's eyes, she felt the pain and humiliation lessen. Although Jamie had known Stephanie for over four years, she'd never felt as close to her as she did now.

"Forget about those losers and hit the dance floor with me," Stephanie encouraged, as she pulled Jamie under the rotating red and white stars which were projected onto the dance floor.

Stephanie spent the next two hours trying to cheer Jamie up. Although Jamie wanted to go home, Stephanie wouldn't allow her to leave. After all, as Stephanie had put it, they wouldn't let those awful boys scare them away.

When the dance finally came to an end, Stephanie waited with Jamie until Mr. Banks picked her up.

"Thanks for everything you've done tonight," Jamie said as she hugged her best friend.

"No problem, Jamie. That's why I'm here."

After arriving home, Jamie couldn't bring herself to tell her parents about what had happened at the dance. Instead, she claimed to have had a wonderful time. Then she hurried to her room and shut the door. She cried a little, still deeply hurt by Craig's actions. However, she was comforted by the thought that Stephanie would always be there for her.

* * *

At school on Monday morning, Jamie wasn't surprised to find that no one was talking about Craig's bet. She knew that all the girls were still embarrassed, and the boys were afraid of getting suspended. Jamie was relieved that the incident was being kept quiet. She wanted to get back to her normal routine and never think about Craig again.

As soon as the bell rang, Jamie hurried to her second class of the day. She had science with Stephanie, and she was eager to see her. For some reason, Jamie couldn't get in touch with Stephanie over the weekend, and she wanted to thank her again for being such a great friend.

Jamie sat down at the table which she and Stephanie always shared. Since she was the first student in the classroom, she spent her free time finishing some homework.

Soon, the classroom was full of students, but the seat beside Jamie was still empty. Expecting Stephanie to walk into the classroom at any moment, Jamie turned around in her seat to look at the door. Suddenly, she gasped. Stephanie was already in the classroom, sitting in the back row. Confused, Jamie waved to Stephanie, but she didn't respond.

When science class ended, Jamie hurried towards Stephanie. "Why didn't you sit with me?" she demanded, deeply hurt by her so-called best friend's behavior.

Stephanie seemed startled that Jamie was talking to her. "Was I supposed to sit with you?" she asked in confusion.

"Yes! You always do!" Jamie cried.

"No, I don't," Stephanie insisted.

Wide-eyed, Jamie looked at Stephanie. "If this is some type of joke, it's not funny. Seriously, why didn't you sit with me?"

"Listen," Stephanie said in annoyance, while standing up. "I don't know who you are or why you want me to sit with you."

"You don't know who I am?" Jamie choked out. "Stephanie, it's me!"

"You may know my name but I don't know yours," Stephanie stated simply. "Now, can you please step aside so I can get to my next class?"

Shocked, Jamie stood still and looked at Stephanie. *What's going on?* she thought as tears stung her eyes.

Impatiently, Stephanie moved around Jamie and then hurried to the classroom's exit. Jamie, on the other hand, made no effort to leave as she watched her best friend disappear through the door.

Jamie didn't see Stephanie again until the last class of the day. For the second time, Stephanie sat far away from her. Throughout the class, Jamie cast glances at Stephanie. At first, Stephanie ignored Jamie's gawking, but she soon grew irritated and began staring back at her in a mocking manner. By the end of the day, Jamie was utterly confused and hurt.

* * *

It was a sunny Saturday mid-morning as Jamie lay on the couch in front of the television.

"I didn't know you liked cartoons," Mrs. Banks said, after entering the living room and looking at the television screen.

"I don't," Jamie snapped.

"Then why have you been watching them for the last two hours?"

"Why are you giving me the third degree?" Jamie yelled, as she harshly turned off the television and stood up. All the anger she'd been holding in for the last few days had finally surfaced.

"Jamie Mel Banks!"

"I'm sorry," Jamie muttered, suddenly feeling ashamed. She knew her mother only used her full name when she was really upset.

"What's troubling you?" Mrs. Banks asked gently in a somewhat nervous tone. "I can tell that something's wrong."

"This is so embarrassing," Jamie said, while avoiding eye contact with her mother. "Remember how I told you and Dad that I had a good time at the dance? Well, that wasn't true. As soon as I got there, I discovered that Craig had nine other dates."

"Why would he do such a thing?" Mrs. Banks asked in shock.

"It was for a bet. If he could get ten dates, he'd win forty dollars."

"Oh, Jamie," Mrs. Banks said as she wrapped her daughter in a hug. "I'm so sorry. Sometimes boys don't mature as quickly as girls, and they just don't realize how their actions hurt other people. Believe me, Jamie, those boys will regret this one day."

"I know, Mom, but that's not my main problem."

"Something worse has happened?" Mrs. Banks asked, with a slight quiver in her voice. She instantly thought back to the day when Jamie had been blessed by Madeline.

"Much worse," Jamie stated. "Stephanie has suddenly forgotten who I am. She pretends that she doesn't even know me!"

"That's absurd!" Mrs. Banks gasped. "You two have been friends for years."

Jamie said nothing. Instead, she lowered her head and tried to force back her tears.

"I'm not sure what's going on," Mrs. Banks began, while thinking this all seemed a bit too odd, "but what I do know is that your father and I will always love you."

"Thanks, Mom," Jamie said with a small smile. "I really needed to hear that."

"That's why I'm here," Mrs. Banks replied as she affectionately smoothed Jamie's hair. "Now, why don't you run upstairs and change out of your pajamas? Your father and I will take you somewhere for lunch."

"Okay," Jamie said, before hurrying up to her bedroom. As she got changed, she began to feel slightly better. She knew that as long as she had her parents, everything would be all right.

Five minutes later, Jamie came down the stairs. She'd expected to see her parents waiting for her at the front door, but they weren't there.

"Mom? Dad?" Jamie called, as she hurried throughout the house. "Where are you?"

No one responded.

They must be in the car waiting for me, Jamie reasoned with relief.

Jamie went outside. Although their car was in the driveway, her parents weren't there. She even checked the backyard, but that was also empty.

They have to be in their bedroom, Jamie thought.

With a racing heart, Jamie re-entered her house. She ran up the stairs and flung her parent's bedroom door open. She felt like crying upon finding that they weren't there either.

Desperate, Jamie picked up the telephone which sat on the bedside table and dialed her father's cell phone number. It didn't even ring but instead went straight to a message which said, "This number is not in service."

"No, no, no," Jamie muttered as she redialed the number, only to get the same message. "This can't be happening."

Hoping that her parents were just playing a mean joke on her, Jamie searched the whole house yet again. She was devastated to discover that she really was the only person there. Jamie collapsed onto the couch and began to sob heartfelt tears. She'd never felt so abandoned and scared in her whole life.

The minutes ticked by slowly, making an hour feel like several days. Finally, Jamie stopped crying and stood up shakily. She had to do something, even if she didn't know what that something was. Jamie quickly decided to look in her parent's bedroom. Maybe they'd left a note for her and she just hadn't seen it.

When Jamie reached her parent's bedroom, it was hard for her to enter. However, something inside of her – perhaps a strength she never knew she had – pushed her forward. She thoroughly searched the bedroom, almost giving up until she came across a small box which was at the bottom of the walk-in closet.

Carefully, Jamie lifted the box and carried it over to the bed. She sat down and then opened the lid, coughing due to the dust. Jamie reached inside and pulled out a dated-looking diary. With slight hesitation, she opened it and began to read.

Dear Diary,   *May 22nd*

It's a girl! I've just returned from the hospital with Sam, and we've learned that our first child will be a girl. After careful consideration, we've decided to name her Jamie Mel Banks. Isn't that such a lovely name, Diary? Jamie is due in four months. I still can't believe that I'll be a mother!

On a similar note, something unusual happened today. While Sam bought us lunch from the hospital's cafeteria, I visited the maternity ward to see all the beautiful newborn babies. They were so cute and precious but very noisy! Anyway, when I was looking at the babies, I saw a new mother, Mrs. Dell, talking to an odd-looking woman who she referred to as Madeline. I overheard Mrs. Dell telling Madeline which baby was hers. A few moments later, Madeline was blessing the baby. After Madeline left, I asked Mrs. Dell what was going on. She said Madeline has supernatural abilities and that she'd just blessed her newborn baby with good fortune. I was very interested in Madeline's work, so I asked for her telephone number. I've told Sam everything, and he's open to the possibility of having Jamie blessed. After all, it can't hurt to try, right?

Jamie paused for a moment to think about what she'd just read. The mere thought of having some strange woman bless her was enough to give her the creeps. She wondered if her parents had actually gone through with the blessing, and if they had, what in the world had possessed them to do so.

Feverishly seeking answers, Jamie continued reading. Most of the following diary entries were about her mother's never-ending pregnancy aches and pains as well as budget-friendly decorating options for Jamie's nursery. Then as her mother's due date drew closer, the entries began to center around her fears and growing anxieties about the pregnancy, Jamie, and life in general. Soon, Jamie's attention was drawn to two disconcerting entries.

Dear Diary, *September 28*th

*I've officially been a mother for ten days! Jamie Mel Banks was born on September 18*th *at 7:10 a.m., weighing seven pounds and five ounces. I went into labor a few days earlier than expected, but the birth went well — or so the doctors say; personally, it felt like fireworks were going off inside of me, and I'm certainly still recovering. The important thing is that Jamie is healthy and safe. However, I just can't help worrying. That's why I called Madeline. She came to our house today and blessed our dear little Jamie in exchange for a small fee. Jamie has been blessed with a happy and carefree life, and that blessing will go into effect when she turns thirteen.*

Dear Diary, *October 30*th

Something horrible has happened! When I was out for a stroll with Jamie, I ran into Mrs. Dell. She was absolutely frantic because she'd heard from several distraught parents that Madeline has been practicing black magic. Rumor has it that all her blessings are twisted to take on different meanings. Sam and I are beside ourselves with worry. We just wanted Jamie to be happy and carefree because we know what it's like to struggle. We've faced so many hardships in life, and I can't imagine Jamie ever having to go through the

16

same thing. So far, Jamie seems fine. All she does is cry, eat, and soil her diapers. Nevertheless, I've never felt so much love for a single human being before. I couldn't stand it if anything ever happened to her. It's just so awful, but I'll go insane if I keep dwelling on Madeline's blessing. I'll forget about it until I can do so no longer – when Jamie turns thirteen. Farewell, Diary.

Jamie's heart raced as she flipped through the rest of the diary. As her mother had promised, the remaining pages were empty.

Something's definitely wrong with Madeline's blessing, Jamie realized with rising panic. *Why didn't my parents just get me christened by a minister?*

Angry and scared, Jamie threw the diary across the room. As she did this, a piece of paper fell from the diary and onto the floor. She quickly retrieved the note and read aloud. "Madeline. 146 Evergreen Circle. 123-5555."

A plan formed in Jamie's mind. If she could get in contact with Madeline, maybe she'd reverse the spell. After all, if Madeline was able to cast such a powerful spell in the first place, Jamie was sure she'd be able to bring back her parents and make Stephanie remember her. It was a longshot and the odds were definitely not in Jamie's favor, but she had to try.

Desperate, Jamie reached for the telephone and dialed Madeline's number. She waited impatiently as the telephone rang several times.

"Hello?" a girl finally answered.

"Madeline?" Jamie asked breathlessly.

"Sorry, you must have the wrong number."

"No!" Jamie shouted, before the girl could hang up. "Please, I need to find Madeline. I know that she lived here at some point."

17

"Maybe," the girl replied, "but I don't know her."

"Do you know anyone who would?" Jamie pleaded.

"I can ask my mom. Hold on a minute."

Jamie waited anxiously for the girl to return to the telephone.

"Madeline lived here before we moved in," the girl said in a somewhat odd tone, after returning to the phone. "She's in jail now."

"What?" Jamie cried.

"She's in jail," the girl repeated slowly. "Mom says Madeline got sentenced to life at Centennial Penitentiary. Whatever she did must have been really bad."

"Thanks so much for your help," Jamie said quickly, before hanging up the phone and then dialing the operator. "I need directions to Centennial Penitentiary," she demanded.

An hour had now passed, and Jamie was still riding her bike as fast as she could towards Centennial Penitentiary. Her legs felt like they each weighed a hundred pounds, and her hands were sweaty and sore from gripping the handlebars in a nervous manner. Jamie was exhausted, but she knew she had to keep on going.

Finally, Jamie arrived at Centennial Penitentiary. She took a moment to catch her breath, while looking upon the jail. It was a large, gray building that featured hundreds of bar-covered windows. Even more daunting was the tall fence topped with barbed wire which surrounded the property.

Jamie secured her bike to a pole before approaching the large, scary-looking gate. Nervously, she pressed a large buzzer and then waited for a response.

"Centennial Penitentiary," a man answered in a deep tone. "Please state your purpose for being here."

"I need to see one of your inmates. Her name is Madeline."

There was a moment of silence. Jamie was just about to repeat herself when the gate suddenly opened.

Uncertain, Jamie carefully walked through the gate. She was met with a security guard who manned the door to the building. The guard said nothing as he swept a handheld metal detector over her body and then directed her inside. The door closed harshly behind Jamie, and she was now alone.

The interior of the building was just as gray as the exterior. The first thing Jamie saw was a long foyer which led to a reception desk. She walked down the hall, and with every step she took, a loud echo followed her. It was an eerie feeling made all the worse by the man at the desk, who stared at her in an odd manner.

"You're here to see Madeline," the man at the desk said, before Jamie even had a chance to say hello.

"Yes," Jamie replied, immediately recognizing his voice from the intercom. She looked at his employee I.D. which read Karl.

"Why do you want to see her?" Karl asked sharply. "You're not a family member or friend, are you?"

"No, but my parents knew Madeline," Jamie explained. "I really need to see her."

"I need to know why," Karl pressed.

Jamie sighed, knowing that she'd have to be honest if she ever hoped to see Madeline. "When I was a baby, Madeline blessed me. Now, her blessing is turning into a curse and it's destroying my life. The only person who can save me is Madeline. Please, I have to see her." Jamie cringed after she'd spoken. She knew she sounded insane.

"I know all about Madeline," Karl said in a stone-cold voice. "Everyone at Centennial Penitentiary does. I've heard weird things about her case – things which made me believe in the supernatural."

"So, can I see her?" Jamie asked hopefully.

"No. Madeline is in solitary confinement. No one is allowed to see her. Centennial Penitentiary can't take the chance of Madeline casting a spell on anyone else."

"Madeline must have prison guards," Jamie challenged. "After all, you wouldn't just lock her up and allow her to die. So, tell me, are her prison guards cursed?"

"Not that we know of," Karl admitted.

"Then I'll take my chances. I want to see Madeline."

"I'm afraid your request has been denied," Karl replied. Sighing slightly, he added, "I understand your predicament, but at least you're still alive – things could've turned out much worse."

"Fine," Jamie snapped, casting Karl an angry glare. As she turned around to leave, she bumped into a woman dressed in a white uniform. "Sorry," she muttered.

"It's okay, honey," the woman replied. "No harm was done."

Jamie watched as the woman hurried through a door marked, *Employees Only*. However, her attention was soon drawn to a large family who had just entered the foyer. They spoke loudly and in upset tones. When they reached the desk, the commotion heightened.

"My daughter doesn't belong in this horrible place!" a woman cried. "She is a good girl!"

Jamie guessed that this was the family of a new inmate, and that the frantic woman was the inmate's mother. As Karl tried to deal with the situation, Jamie used the distraction to her advantage. Acting quickly, she hunched slightly and then hurried through the employee's entrance.

Now in a brightly-lit hallway, Jamie quickly read the signs on different doors, praying to find an unattended administrative office which would somehow direct her towards Madeline's jail cell. It had just occurred to her that she had no clue where she was going or even what Madeline looked like.

Jamie was unable to find any such office containing a map or the inmate's files. Instead, she found herself outside the kitchen. She checked her watch, which read 1:30 p.m. Jamie peeked inside the kitchen and, seeing that it was empty, she entered.

Quickly, Jamie searched the kitchen. "Bingo!" she said louder than intended, as she pulled a white uniform from an open closet. If she was going to be walking around these hallways, she'd better look like she belonged. Hurriedly, Jamie put the uniform on, making sure to gather all her hair underneath the white hat. Grabbing an empty tray for appearance's sake, she headed out of the kitchen.

Jamie walked down the hallway, mimicking the confidence of a seasoned employee. Only her eyes told the truth as they darted nervously back and forth. Finally, Jamie reached the end of the hallway. She wasn't sure if she was relieved or scared to see that this was where the jail cells began.

"Hello," Jamie said in her most mature tone, greeting the security guard who manned the entrance. "I'm here to collect the dirty dishes."

The security guard opened the door for Jamie, glancing at her as she walked past. He said nothing, but she could feel his eyes on her as she continued forward.

Jamie looked into the jail cells, surprised to see many of the inmates reading books and seemingly completing homework. They appeared uninterested in her presence.

"I wonder who pays for their education," Jamie muttered, shivering at the thought of educated criminals.

Her attention was soon drawn to an old man with long white hair, who sat still and silently in his cell. His gray eyes burrowed into hers, chilling her in the process. Slowly, with one long, crooked finger, he gestured for her to come closer.

Jamie gulped nervously, but nonetheless she stepped forward.

"You just got hired?" the man asked, as he stood up with difficulty and then walked shakily towards her.

"Excuse me?"

"I haven't seen you before," the man added with a mischievous smile.

"I'm looking for Madeline," Jamie said quickly. "Do you know where I can find her?"

The man suddenly looked concerned. "She's over there – behind those doors," the man finally replied, while pushing his thin arm through the bars and pointing towards large doors marked, *No Entry*.

"Thank you," Jamie said sincerely as she began to walk away.

"Whatever your business with her is, it isn't worth it," the man warned. "She's very dangerous. Do you see the man in the jail cell beside me?"

Jamie squinted in search of the prisoner in the neighboring jail cell. "I don't see anyone," she answered.

"That's because Madeline got to him."

Jamie gulped, but she continued forward. As she opened the heavy doors, her heart raced.

"Who's there?" a creepy voice immediately demanded.

The room was much darker than the rest of Centennial Penitentiary. It took several moments for Jamie's eyes to adjust to the sudden change in light. Even when her eyes were accustomed to the dimness, Jamie had trouble seeing Madeline. Through the thick bars, all she could make out was a dark figure sitting hunched in a chair.

"Who's there?" Madeline demanded in a much harsher tone. "Come closer."

Jamie refused to budge. Instead, she watched as Madeline stood up and proceeded towards her. She gasped as Madeline was illuminated by a small light from above. She was a very short woman with poor posture. Her long black hair, which perfectly matched her creepy eyes, was styled in old-fashioned ringlets that concealed most of her face. Like all the other inmates, she wore a dark orange jumpsuit. However, the hue of her clothes appeared much deeper and almost blood-like.

"Ah!" Madeline said so quickly and loudly that Jamie jumped in surprise. "You're Jamie Banks – the girl I blessed thirteen years ago."

"That's...that's right," Jamie said with a gulp, "but I wouldn't really call it a blessing."

"I *blessed* you," Madeline interrupted, before Jamie could say another word. "Yet, I cannot deny that my blessing was rather ironic. You see, Jamie, your parents wanted you to be happy and carefree. Unfortunately, your parent's wish was an oxymoron – one cannot be carefree if they are to be happy. To be carefree is to be dead, and to be happy is to be alive. Do you understand my dilemma? I could never wish you dead nor make you immortal. No, I could never do that. Instead, I blessed you with ironic happiness. This means that you would experience happiness only to have it taken away. When people say something's too good to be true, they're right, Jamie."

"Well, that explains what's been happening to me," Jamie muttered, trying not to glare at Madeline. "Is there anything I can do to reverse my parent's wish?"

"A wish cannot be altered," Madeline answered.

"Not even thirteen years later?" Jamie asked hopefully.

"Not even thirteen seconds later."

"There has to be a way..." Jamie began to say. However, she was interrupted as two men barged into the room.

"That's her!" Karl shouted.

Jamie watched in horror as the security guard, who manned the entrance to the jail cells, grabbed her shoulders.

"I thought she looked suspicious," the security guard said.

"Let me go!" Jamie cried as she struggled in his grasp.

"You were told to leave," Karl replied. "You shouldn't be in here."

"I had to see Madeline." Jamie looked desperately at Madeline, who was now hunched in a corner of the jail cell. "She's the only one who can help me."

"Only you can help yourself," Madeline said in a creepy manner.

"Get her out of here," Karl instructed the security guard, obviously afraid for the safety of them all.

"No!" Jamie yelled, as she struggled out of the security guard's grasp and ran towards Madeline's jail cell. "Can I make a wish?" she begged.

"Of course," Madeline replied with a smile.

"I wish that my parent's wish was never granted. I want to be a normal teenager who experiences happiness as well as hardship."

"Get the girl out of here now!" Karl demanded, more frantic than ever.

The security guard grabbed Jamie's arm, but this time she didn't retaliate. She knew she'd done everything humanely possible to save herself.

After returning the cook's uniform and being told never to come back, Jamie was escorted out of Centennial Penitentiary. Praying that Madeline had granted her wish without any negative consequences, Jamie peddled as fast as she could towards her house.

When Jamie finally arrived home, everything was quiet. She stood in the seemingly empty house, devastated that Madeline hadn't granted her wish.

"Jamie Mel Banks!" someone suddenly called.

Almost breathlessly, Jamie watched as her parents emerged from the living room. Although they looked simultaneously concerned and angry, they were most definitely alive and well.

"Where have you been?" Mrs. Banks scolded.

"I..." Jamie tried to answer.

"We've been waiting for you," Mr. Banks interrupted. "We were meant to be going out for lunch, remember?"

"I know, but I had to…"

"We were very concerned," Mrs. Banks interrupted this time.

As her mother lectured her about the importance of being reliable and always telling them where she was, Jamie tried to hide her smile. She'd never been so happy to see her parents.

* * *

It was a sunny Saturday morning, and Jamie was heading out of her house, on route to the park so she could enjoy the beautiful day. As she locked the door behind her, she smiled happily.

Over a week had passed since Jamie visited Madeline at Centennial Penitentiary, and her life had returned to normal. Craig apologized to Jamie and the rest of the girls, and he even gave back the money he'd won from the bet. More importantly, Stephanie remembered who Jamie was, and she was eager to resume their friendship.

As Jamie walked down her driveway and then turned the corner, she almost collided with the mailman. "Oops," she said, with an apologetic smile.

"Hello, Jamie," the mailman greeted, not the least bit annoyed. "I was just on my way to your house. There's only one letter today, and it's addressed to you."

"Thanks," Jamie said, taking the letter from the nosey but nonetheless pleasant mailman. "Have a nice day."

When Jamie was alone, she looked at the envelope. There was no return address and she didn't recognize the scrappy handwriting. Curiously, she tore open the letter, and then she almost fainted. It was an invoice from Madeline for the amount of $19.95.

* * *

The Amazing Amber Cook

"Who is that?" sixteen-year-old Shane Radway asked his best friend, Drew Harris.

Drew looked up from his notebook to follow Shane's stare. He saw a girl who wore ripped jeans and a blue baby tee which read, "Rebel" in large red letters. The girl was undeniably pretty, but her most striking feature was her red hair which was almost as bright as the writing on her baby tee.

"I don't know who she is," Drew replied as he adjusted his thick black rimmed glasses and resumed writing in his notebook.

"Well, I'm going to find out," Shane said confidently as he brushed his dark brown hair out of his eyes and proceeded towards the new girl.

"Hey, I'm Shane Radway," he introduced himself with a wide smile. "I haven't seen you before. Are you new to the school?"

"I've just moved to Maple Hitch – you do the math," the girl replied, not bothering to look at Shane. Instead, she continued to browse the school library's bookshelves. Her tone was calm and perhaps a bit insulting, but it wasn't completely unfriendly.

When Shane saw the girl smirk slightly, he instantly took it as a sign that she wanted the conversation to continue. "What's your name?" he pressed.

"Why do you want to know?" she asked, finally looking at Shane.

Shane immediately noticed her eyes which were the brightest shade of emerald green he had ever seen. "I want to know your name so I can invite you to sit with me and my friend, Drew."

The girl seemed to consider Shane's answer for a moment and then she smiled. "My name's Amber Cook."

"Would you like to join us, Amber Cook?" Shane asked with a friendly smile.

"I guess it's your lucky day," Amber answered before walking towards the desk and flinging her backpack onto the table. "Hey, Drew," she said confidently.

"Hi," Drew replied, glancing at her for a mere second before returning his attention to his notebook.

Amber retrieved books from her backpack and began working on a school assignment. They studied together in silence until she let out a frustrated sigh.

"Can I borrow your pencil sharpener?" Amber asked Drew while holding up her broken pencil. She didn't wait for an answer as she leaned towards him and took it. "The first answer is wrong," she said casually, after stealing a glance at his math book.

Drew looked up in shock. "Excuse me?"

"Drew's something of a math prodigy," Shane explained to Amber. "He never makes mistakes."

"That's right," Drew said, defending his title. "Besides, how would you know? You hardly had time to read the question, far less answer it."

Amber just shook her head. "You made a very common yet simple mistake. In this type of equation, you have to convert the number to a percent-percentage before calculating the total."

"I didn't make a mistake!"

"Yes, you did," Amber replied calmly. "The answer is 293700 – not 29370."

"Why don't you check the answers at the back of the book?" Shane suggested, before Drew could say anything else. He knew how defensive Drew could get and he didn't want him offending their new friend.

"Fine, I will," Drew said haughtily as he flipped to the back of the math book.

As Shane watched the color drain from Drew's face, he knew that Amber's answer was the correct one.

"How...how did you know that?" Drew stuttered. "How could you have possibly answered such a long equation in a matter of seconds?"

"I guess I'm the real math prodigy around here," Amber said with a confident laugh as she grabbed her books and backpack from the table and then walked away without saying goodbye.

The bell had just rung, but Drew made no effort to move.

"Aren't you coming?" Shane urged, secretly hoping to catch up to Amber.

"It's impossible," Drew muttered, still in shock.

"She's probably already taken the same math course and just remembered the answer," Shane reassured his friend. "Now, come on or we'll be late."

Drew wasn't satisfied with Shane's explanation. *What are the odds of remembering an answer to a random math question right down to the last zero?* he wondered as they hurried to class.

31

Shane and Drew were a few minutes late entering gym class that day. However, it didn't matter since no one was paying attention to them. Instead, everyone in the class was focused on the heated debate that was taking place between the gym teacher, Mr. Ingles, and a familiar-looking red haired girl.

"That's not the best way to hold a badminton racquet," Amber argued.

"Ms. Cook, I've been teaching students how to play badminton for over six years!" Mr. Ingles bellowed. "I know how to hold a racquet!"

"I'm not saying you can't hold a racquet," Amber replied calmly, as if she was the one in authority. "I'm just saying you're not holding it in the most effective way."

Although Amber didn't appear the least bit flustered, Mr. Ingles looked outraged. His face was a deep shade of red and beads of sweat rolled down his forehead.

"I don't mean to emasculate you – I just want to show you a better way," Amber said sweetly as she removed the badminton racquet from Mr. Ingles' hand.

Amber's comment was met with a mixture of laughter and shock from the students. Shane and Drew merely looked at each other in bewilderment.

"Hit the birdie to me, Mr. Ingles," Amber instructed as she ran backwards.

Shane's eyes widened as he saw Amber heading blindly towards a basketball that lay on the floor behind her. He didn't have a chance to warn her as she quickly jumped backwards over the basketball. Shane looked at his classmates, wondering if they had seen Amber's perfectly coordinated backwards jump. Apparently they hadn't, since they were too busy staring at Mr. Ingles, whose face was becoming redder as the seconds passed.

"Hit the birdie to me!" Amber called again, once she was far away from Mr. Ingles.

In confusion and shock, Mr. Ingles served the birdie to Amber. She returned the serve with a move that was the opposite of what Mr. Ingles had always taught. The birdie flew so fast that when Mr. Ingles swung his badminton racquet in response, the birdie had already landed on the floor.

"See, I told you my technique was better," Amber said with a superior smile.

At the end of gym class, Shane and Drew saw Mr. Ingles pull Amber aside. "We need to have a little chat," they heard their teacher say.

"Okay," Amber replied casually, while looking at her watch. "I can only give you three minutes of my time though."

Mr. Ingles' eyes widened with surprise. He finally sighed, as if deciding to ignore her latest comment. "We need to discuss what happened in gym class today. Although your badminton technique was surprisingly good, the way in which you displayed your talent was unacceptable."

Amber looked confused by Mr. Ingles comment, but then she smiled in understanding. "I apologize for embarrassing you."

Shane and Drew hurried out of the gym, trying desperately to conceal their laughter. The look of complete shock on Mr. Ingles' face and Amber's dignified strut out of the gym was too much for them to bear.

* * *

It was only 7:30 the next morning as Shane walked along the empty corridors of Maple Hitch High School. In the silence, his mind wandered to thoughts of Amber. Truthfully, he hadn't stopped thinking about her. There was something so different and alluring about Amber. It was as if she was drawing him in and refusing to let go.

"Amber?" Shane said in shock as he turned a corner and almost collided with her.

Amber looked startled to see another student in the school. "What are you doing here?" she demanded.

"Drew's getting his wisdom teeth pulled today, so I'm collecting his homework before class," Shane explained. He suddenly looked at Amber's top with wide eyes. "You're not allowed to wear that in school," he warned her.

Amber looked down at her baby blue tank top that read, "School Stinks" in white sparkly lettering. "What's wrong with my top?"

"Nothing," Shane replied quickly. "It's just that tank tops aren't allowed to be worn on school property."

"Would it offend the school if I wore the tank top on my head?" Amber asked with a loud laugh. "I really couldn't care less about school rules."

"Okay," Shane replied, not sure what else to say. "So, do you like Maple Hitch High so far?"

Amber had just opened her mouth to reply when someone interrupted her.

"Are you Amber Cook?" a tall boy with dark brown hair asked.

Oh no, Shane thought upon seeing Mr. Ingles' son, Lance. *This can't be good.*

"Who wants to know?" Amber shot back.

"I want to know," Lance sneered. "You must be Amber – your attitude gives you away."

"In the flesh," Amber admitted, raising her hands in the air as if her presence was a blessing.

"My dad was right – you are a cocky narcissist."

"And your father would be..." Amber said, placing her hands on her hips.

"Mr. Ingles."

Amber looked seriously at Lance for a moment and then laughed. "Sorry."

"Although that wasn't a very convincing apology, I'll accept it," Lance offered. "But I want you to apologize to my father in front of the whole gym class today."

"You've misunderstood me," Amber replied with a high pitch laugh. "I meant I'm sorry Mr. Ingles is your father. He can't stand anyone telling him that he's wrong. It must be hard for you to live with someone like that."

Shane watched as Lance's face went bright red. *Lance inherited his father's inability to hide emotions,* he thought.

"What did you just say?" Lance bellowed.

"You heard me," Amber scolded, obviously not fazed by Lance's powerful voice.

"I don't hit girls, but I'll make an exception for you," Lance seethed.

"You'll get expelled if you hit someone on school property," Shane pointed out in a shaky voice, trying to save Amber from Lance's wrath.

Amber let out another high pitch laugh before Lance could say anything. "Then we'll go outside," she offered.

Shane couldn't believe his ears. All the students in Maple Hitch High School were afraid of Lance.

"You actually want to fight me?" Lance asked, also looking surprised.

"Sure. Why not? We have half an hour before class begins."

"Let's go," Lance said, storming down the hallway.

"Coming, honey!" Amber called mockingly.

"Wait!" Shane cried, grabbing Amber's arm. He was shocked to feel how cold it was. However, he had more important things to worry about than Amber's temperature; he was more concerned about her mere survival. "You can't fight Lance. He'll kill you!"

Amber rolled her eyes. "I'd laugh if I wasn't so bored."

"Why don't you understand?"

"I understand just fine. Do you want to watch me wipe the pavement with Lance's face?"

"No!" Shane gasped. "You scare me when you talk like this."

"Don't worry. We're friends, and I'd never hurt you. Now, come on. It's not polite to keep Lance waiting."

Shane followed Amber outside and then off the school's property. Normally, he'd never encourage a fight by watching it. However, Amber's high level of self-confidence made him extremely curious.

"It's customary to shake hands before fighting," Amber told Lance as she offered her hand to him. "We wouldn't want to forget our etiquette, would we?"

Lance's expression seemed to change as he shook Amber's hand. He looked as if he'd just been stunned.

At lightning speed, Amber took her hand away from Lance's and then placed it on his shoulder.

With the strength of only one hand, she shoved Lance backwards. He slammed against a tree with a sickening thud.

"Either you apologize to me or I'll start playing really rough," Amber threatened in a stone cold voice.

Lance's eyes were wild with fear. "Okay, okay. I'm sorry. Please don't hurt me."

"That's better," Amber said.

Lance cast Amber a horrified look and then, stumbling slightly, ran back to the school.

"See?" Amber said confidently, turning towards Shane and wiping her hands. "I won without even hurting him."

"I don't know about that," Shane confessed, still amazed by Amber's super strength. "I think you permanently bruised Lance's ego!"

Amber shrugged as if she didn't care. "Why don't we get Drew's homework together?" she asked before linking arms with Shane.

Shane said nothing as Amber dragged him around every one of Drew's classes. Soon, they had collected all his homework.

"Poor Drew," Shane said while looking at the homework. "There must be a hundred pages here."

"Excuse me, young lady!" someone called suddenly.

Shane looked up to see Maple Hitch High's principal, Mr. Kannon, hurrying towards them.

"Yeah," Amber replied while looking at the principal. "Can I help you with something?"

Mr. Kannon looked shocked by Amber's words. "Yes," he replied in a stern voice. "I'm afraid that tank tops are banned from our school. You must change immediately."

"I don't have another top," Amber told the principal. "Do you want to get ice cream after school?" she asked, turning to Shane and ignoring Mr. Kannon in the process.

"Um, I...I think Mr. Kannon is still talking to you," Shane stuttered, completely bewildered by Amber's behavior.

"Oh, are you still here?" she asked, turning around to face Mr. Kannon once again. "I told you I don't have another top."

Mr. Kannon placed his thumb and index finger on his forehead as if he had a bad headache. "I'm presuming you're new since I haven't seen you before. However, you can't act in such a disrespectful manner. You attend Maple Hitch High School now, and you have to abide by our rules."

"I'm not going to follow stupid rules," Amber shot back.

"Excuse me?" Mr. Kannon said in shock.

"Leave me alone. I'm talking to my friend."

"No, you are not. You're coming with me." The principal pointed down the hallway. "Follow me."

Amber rolled her eyes but followed Mr. Kannon anyway. "I'll see you in class!" she called back to Shane.

"She's nuts," Shane said out loud as he watched them walk away. "She's completely nuts."

Shane didn't see Amber for the rest of the day. In fact, he didn't see her the following day either. A week passed, but Amber still hadn't returned to school. Finally, Shane presumed that she'd been expelled.

Shane was actually starting to miss Amber. Although she was rude and disrespectful towards people in authority, she also had an unbelievable amount of spunk and was unlike anyone else he'd ever met.

* * *

It was a cool morning in the middle of September as Shane leaned against the wall of his house and waited for Drew. He had agreed to help Drew choose a gift for his younger sister and had even made a list of suggestions.

"Hey, Shane!" Drew called as he jogged towards the Radway's house. "I'm glad you're helping me out. I have no clue what to get Susan. Seriously, how many twelve year olds don't have a birthday wish list?"

"I wonder what your parents did to deserve two weird kids," Shane said with a laugh.

Drew glared at Shane and then laughed. "It takes a weirdo to know a weirdo."

"Okay. Enough nonsense," Shane said, getting down to business. "I've made a list of things Susan will probably like. What about a magic set?"

"A magic set?" Drew repeated while wrinkling his nose. "I don't know. She's turning thirteen – not six."

"Alright," Shane said, crossing that item off the list. "How about the latest City Wars video game?"

"That's just a silly point-and-shoot game. There's no way she'd like that."

"Fine," Shane sighed, crossing another item off the list.

"How about a make-up set?" a familiar voice, which came from behind Shane and Drew, suggested.

They turned around to see Amber standing there.

"Hi," she said casually. "I heard you guys talking about getting a gift for a thirteen-year-old girl. She'd probably like a make-up set that has eye shadow, lip gloss and nail polish."

"You were listening to our conversation?" Drew snapped at Amber, before Shane could say anything.

"Yeah," she replied casually once again, "but not intentionally. When I saw you, I ran after you and accidentally overheard the conversation."

"I didn't hear you running behind me," Drew said suspiciously.

"What's your problem, Drew? If it's with me, you should let me know now."

"Please don't fight," Shane interjected. "It doesn't matter how you heard our conversation. The important thing is that we get a good gift for Susan."

"I suppose so," Drew agreed grumpily. "Where do you get a make-up set?"

Amber let out an amused laugh. "Boys are hopeless!"

"Not so hopeless that we can't figure out you've been missing for quite some time," Shane pointed out. "What happened?"

"At first I was only suspended for talking back to the principal, but then the incident with Lance Ingles got me expelled," Amber replied, rolling her eyes.

"What incident?" Drew asked in confusion.

"Shane didn't tell you?" Amber asked with a little smirk. "I fought Lance."

"You what?" Drew cried. "Lance has been acting differently, but I haven't seen a black eye or anything like that."

"You have a lot to learn about me," Amber told Drew. "The damage I inflict is much more painful than physical wounds."

"What...what do you mean by that?" Drew stuttered, absolutely shocked by Amber's words.

Amber didn't answer. Instead, she smiled.

"Thanks for the advice on Susan's gift, but don't feel like you have to stick around," Drew said as bravely as possible. "If you tell me what store I can buy it in..."

"Are you trying to get rid of me?" Amber asked angrily.

"Not exactly," Drew lied.

"It's lucky for Drew that he's your friend," Amber said seriously as she turned towards Shane. "I would never hurt a friend of yours, even if I wanted to."

"What do you mean by that?" Drew demanded for the second time that day.

"You're meant to be the math prodigy – do the equation and figure it out," Amber mocked. "We'll hang out sometime soon," she promised Shane as she finally took Drew's hint and left.

"She's crazy!" Drew shrieked, once Amber had disappeared down the street. "She just threatened to hurt me – she's completely nuts. Why in the world does she like you so much?"

"Calm down, Drew. Amber won't really hurt you. When she fought Lance, she didn't hurt him. She just startled him."

"Lance is so tall. How could Amber survive a fight with him in the first place?"

"Easily. Lance didn't even have a chance to touch her."

"I'm telling you, Shane," Drew said seriously, "that girl is really weird. I think you should stay away from her."

Shane didn't respond, but he did take his friend's words seriously. *Is Amber actually a threat to me?* he wondered.

* * *

It was Monday afternoon as Shane and Drew walked home from school.

"I'll have to pretend I'm sick tomorrow, if I don't get all my English homework done," Drew said through a sigh. "Does Ms. Mackellar really think it's humanly possible to write a six page essay in one night?"

"I'm glad Mr. Ellis is my English teacher. His idea of homework is watching a movie that's based on a novel."

"Lucky you," Drew said with a groan.

"See you later," Shane said with a sympathetic smile before they parted ways.

Drew was so wrapped up in thoughts about his English assignment that he jumped when someone called his name.

"Drew!" a female voice called again, this time much closer and sharper.

Startled, Drew turned around. His heart rate increased when he saw Amber. There was just something about her that freaked him out.

"We need to talk," Amber said quickly. "I've been keeping a secret from you and Shane."

Drew looked at Amber with wide eyes. "Go on," he urged, equally surprised and scared by her words.

"I'm an alien."

Drew looked at Amber, expecting her to start laughing hysterically. His heart raced faster as she remained emotionless.

"Say that again," Drew demanded breathlessly, thinking he may have misheard Amber.

"I'm an alien who has traveled from Jupiter."

"How...how is that possible? There's no oxygen on Jupiter and it's unbelievably cold. How could you survive?"

"There's been life on Jupiter since dinosaurs roamed Earth. All the aliens on Jupiter are cold blooded and can breathe underwater, on Earth and in the solar system. I assure you that life on Jupiter is plausible and actually quite enjoyable."

"If what you're saying is true, how could you travel to Earth? Jupiter is five hundred and eighty eight million kilometers away!"

"You know the solar system well," Amber said with a smirk. "My species have been traveling to Earth for centuries. It's usually someone older who is sent to Earth, but I won the First Official Contest to Earth for Teenagers."

"No way," Drew said, shaking his head. "You have to be kidding."

Amber's eyes looked wild with anger. "How dare you not believe me!"

Suddenly, Amber closed her eyes and became eerily quiet.

Drew heard a low buzzing noise coming from Amber. Then he almost fainted as two green antennas grew out of her head.

"Believe me now?" Amber asked, wiggling her antennas.

With his mouth wide open, Drew nodded. He was in too much shock to say anything.

"Listen up," Amber began harshly. "You're putting a lot of strain on my friendship with Shane. I should just zap you into infinity, but I won't. Instead, I'll send you to Jupiter. You can wait there while Shane and I spend some quality time together. Then, once I have convinced Shane to return to Jupiter with me, we'll reunite with you and perhaps all become friends."

"Why would you want me to live on Jupiter?"

"You and Shane are such good friends," Amber said with a frustrated sigh. "I wouldn't want to upset him. Does Shane have a good relationship with his family?" she asked, after a few seconds of silence. "Maybe I should also bring them to Jupiter."

"Why are you doing this?" Drew cried. "Why do you care about Shane so much?"

"Shane's so cute," Amber gushed, "and he stands by me like my so-called friends on Jupiter never would."

"Your devotion is touching," Drew said in a disgusted tone. "But you've forgotten one important element – humans can't survive on Jupiter."

"Don't worry about that. I have it all taken care of."

"How?"

"You're on a need-to-know basis. And this, my friend, is something that you don't need to know."

Drew began to walk backwards. *She's seriously evil,* he realized as he turned around and ran.

Since Drew's back was to Amber, he never saw the electrical currents that pulsated in between her antennas. He also didn't see the lightning bolt that shot from her antennas and straight towards him. All Drew knew was that a cold sensation was surging throughout his body and that he was no longer on Earth.

Ding Dong. Ding Dong. Ding Dong.

Amber stood impatiently outside the Radway's small house and rang the doorbell repeatedly.

"May I help you?" Mrs. Radway asked in an annoyed tone, after she'd opened the door.

"Is Shane home?" Amber asked quickly and rudely.

"Who are you?"

"Amber."

"Shane's talked about you," Mrs. Radway said knowingly. "Come in," she added in a more friendly tone. "I'll tell him you're here."

Amber stepped inside as Mrs. Radway left in search of Shane. She immediately noticed the faded furniture that looked like it came from a thrift store. She felt like recommending a consignment store that offered newer furniture. However, she kept her mouth shut because she didn't want to insult Shane. The process of thinking before speaking was new for Amber.

"Hey, Amber," Shane greeted as he came down the stairs.

"Do you want to go for a walk?" she suggested.

"Right now?" Shane asked with uncertainty. "It's cold and late."

"That's exactly how I like it." Noting Shane's reluctant look, she added, "I have something really important to tell you."

"Okay," Shane gave in as he opened the hallway closet and retrieved his jacket. "I'm going for a walk with Amber!" he called to his mother before hurrying out of the house.

Silence followed Shane and Amber as they walked along the deserted street.

"What do you have to tell me?" Shane asked, finally breaking the silence. He was worried that something was really wrong.

"I haven't been completely honest with you," Amber said slowly and anxiously. "I'm not just new to Maple Hitch – I'm actually new to Earth as well."

Shane stared at Amber and then began to laugh.

"I'm not kidding!" Amber said irritably. "I'm an alien from Jupiter and I've come to take you back with me." She waited for Shane to say something, but when he failed to speak, she continued. "Jupiter's really amazing. There's so much to do, and you can even visit other planets. You'll also have Drew and me there."

Shane gave Amber a funny look. "You can drop the act now."

"I'm not acting. I'm really an alien," Amber protested. "I have the power to transport us to Jupiter right now. We can even bring Mr. Ingles, Mr. Kannon and anyone else we don't like. Then we'll cast them into space and watch them float away. What do you say, Shane? It would be so much fun!"

"You're horrible!" Shane cried suddenly.

"What?" Amber shrieked, not liking what she'd just heard.

"I said you're horrible! If you're not an evil alien, then you're a crazy human – either way, you scare me. I wouldn't go to the mall with you, far less Jupiter. Do me a favor and get some psychiatric help."

With that said, Shane turned around and hurried away.

"Shane!" Amber wailed. "You don't mean it!"

"Stay away from me!" Shane shouted, starting to run.

When Shane finally reached his house, he opened the door and then slammed it shut behind him. He leaned against the locked door, all the while thinking about Amber's terrifying words.

How could I have been so wrong about her? Shane thought with a shiver.

Ring. Ring.

"I'm back! I'll get it!" Shane yelled as he ran to the phone. He hoped it was Drew. He needed to tell him how crazy Amber was and that they had to stay away from her. However, he was extremely disappointed and even frightened when he heard Amber's voice.

"We have to talk," Amber begged. "I really want to take you to Jupiter."

"What part of leave me alone don't you understand?" Shane cried.

"Please come with me."

"No!"

"Fine!" Amber cried angrily. "If you refuse to come with me, I won't return Drew. I will, however, bring my wrath upon Earth."

Suddenly, the phone went dead. Amber had hung up.

Quickly, Shane dialed Drew's number. The phone seemed to ring forever.

"Hello?" someone finally answered the phone.

"Drew?" Shane asked breathlessly.

"Do I sound like a teenage boy?" Mrs. Harris asked with a chuckle. "Drew isn't home yet. I thought he was still with you. He's probably at the ice cream parlor again. I swear, he either spends his money on math textbooks or ice cream – never anything else!"

Shane forced himself to laugh politely. "Can you ask him to call me when he gets home?"

"Of course. Have a nice night, Shane."

Shane hung up the telephone and waited by it all night. He had almost fallen asleep in his chair when the telephone rang at 11:45 PM.

"Hello?" he answered.

"Shane," Mrs. Harris said tearfully. "Drew hasn't come home. Where is he?"

"I...I don't know, but I think I know who's responsible."

Mrs. Harris had come over to the Radway's house on that awful night three weeks ago. Shane had told Mrs. Harris and his parents about his horrifying conversation with Amber. They, along with the police, who were notified twenty four hours later, searched frantically for Drew and Amber. Unfortunately, they found nothing. Even the telephone number and address that Maple Hitch High School had on file for Amber was incorrect. It seemed as if she'd disappeared off the face of the Earth.

* * *

It was a cool day in late October as Shane walked home from school. This was the first day in three weeks that Mrs. Radway had allowed him to walk home alone. Mrs. Radway had become extremely paranoid that Amber would return for Shane and, much to his mortification, had insisted that she accompany Shane to and from school.

Obviously, Shane thought his mother was being too overprotective, but now that he was alone on the darkening, windy street, he had a weird feeling that something bad was about to happen.

"Hey, Shane, remember me?" a chilling voice asked.

Shane turned around slowly, not wanting to confirm his suspicion of who was standing behind him.

"Amber," Shane said with a shiver.

"In the flesh," she said with a big smile.

Shane's skin crawled. The last time he'd heard Amber speak those words was just before she fought Lance. Fearing that Amber was a threat to his life, he turned around and ran.

Shane gasped when Amber appeared in front of him. Quickly, he ran in the opposite direction, but once again, there she was. Shane watched in fear as Amber closed her eyes. A buzzing noise followed and then two green antennas grew from her head.

"They're great for getting clear television reception," Amber joked, pointing to her antennas.

"Please don't hurt me!" Shane cried.

A look of confusion crossed over Amber's face. "Hurt you? Why would you think that? I would never hurt you!"

"But you would hurt Drew, wouldn't you?" Shane pried.

"I *could* have hurt Drew," Amber corrected him. "But I didn't. He's actually having the time of his life in Jupiter. He especially loves sliding on Jupiter's ring, Halo."

"You...you really are an alien."

"You've finally figured it out!" Amber remarked sarcastically. "It took you long enough."

"What do you want with Drew and me?" Shane demanded shakily.

"Your time. Your friendship. If you only knew how lonely I am on Jupiter, you'd be more supportive of my actions. No one likes me on Jupiter. They all say I'm rude. You're the only one who actually likes me."

"If they don't like you, then it's their loss," Shane said, trying to act like a loyal and caring friend. He had quickly decided that it was better to have Amber as his friend than his enemy. "You may challenge authority, but that can be a good trait if the person in authority is influencing others in a bad way. I know for a fact that if Mr. Ingles embarrassed me in front of the class, you'd be the first person to stick up for me. You're loyal, Amber. I can honestly pledge to that."

"Yes!" Amber cried. "You're the only one who sees the true me. Oh, come with me to Jupiter. We could be so happy together."

"Amber, I'm not going to leave Earth for anyone, even you. I'm sorry, but I just can't."

"You *will* come with me," Amber threatened with fiery eyes. "I spared the Earth from my wrath for your sake, Shane. So, if you won't do as I say, why should I protect you from the pain that you're inflicting upon me?"

"Just bring Drew back to Earth and leave us all alone. You can't win."

"Can't I?" Amber said with a smirk. "We'll just see about that."

"Amber, no!" Shane yelled as a spark ignited between her antennas and then engulfed her until she disappeared from his sight.

Shane tried to run away as a whirlwind of sparks surrounded him. His body tingled with a cold sensation until he felt as if he couldn't move or even breathe. He was about to collapse when everything suddenly stopped.

Blackness surrounded Shane. The air was very heavy and cold, but as the seconds passed, he found himself adjusting to the extreme conditions. It was the weirdest feeling he'd ever experienced.

In the darkness, Shane began to walk slowly and cautiously. His feet felt as if they weighed a hundred pounds, but the more he walked, the lighter they became. Shane was also dizzy, but that soon passed too. Even his vision was improving. He was now able to maneuver through the strange place with some success.

I'm in a room, Shane realized, noting that it was colored in an unusual shade of dark green and brown. The room was bare, and there were two doors at opposite ends.

Shane proceeded to the nearest door and opened it. A strong gust of wind almost pulled him through, but he resisted it by holding on tightly to the doorframe. As the suction began to ease, Shane looked out and gasped. In front of him was the most beautiful view he'd ever seen. For miles lay a peaceful scene of blackness and twinkling yellow stars. Shane felt the overwhelming urge to jump out the door and swim in the starry sky. Before forcing himself backwards, he took a long last look and then shut the door.

Shane hurried to the other door and opened it carefully. What was behind the second door was more shocking than the first.

There, having the time of his life, was Drew. He was with three teenage aliens who had green antennas on their heads. The three aliens, as well as Drew, sat around a table quizzing each other. Shane heard one of the aliens ask Drew a long math question. The excitement on Drew's face was apparent.

He loves it here, Shane realized.

Shane was suddenly overwhelmed with a huge moral dilemma. He didn't know if he should sacrifice himself in hopes of saving Earth from Amber's wrath or try to escape and save himself. Either way, he felt doomed.

"I'm so glad you've joined me, Shane," a happy voice said from behind him.

Shane spun around to see Amber with a wide smile on her face. He suddenly wondered what he'd ever seen in her.

"I assume you'll be staying," Amber implied.

"I'll stay," Shane said impulsively. "But only if you leave Earth alone. Promise me that you won't hurt any humans."

"I promise," Amber said as she embraced Shane.

"And," Shane began, pulling away from Amber, "you have to return Drew to Earth."

"Sure," Amber replied. "But I don't know if he'll want to go home. Like I said earlier, he loves it here." She grabbed Shane's hand and led him towards Drew.

Drew's eyes lit up when he saw Shane. "Oh my gosh!" he cried, running towards his friend. "I'm so glad you're here!"

"Do you want to go home?" Shane asked Drew, while looking seriously into his friend's eyes.

"What?" Drew asked with an uncertain smile. "You mean we get to go home? I thought I was stuck here forever!"

"So, you *do* want to go home?" Shane asked, making sure that he understood Drew's feelings clearly.

"Of course," Drew replied passionately. "Jupiter is such a cool place. I'll remember it forever, but I want to go back to Earth and be with my family. I can't imagine how worried my mother must be."

"You're going home then."

"Great! Come on, let's go." Drew tugged on Shane's arm and then looked puzzled when he refused to follow. "Aren't you coming?"

"No," Shane replied sadly. "If I stay here, Amber will let you go and leave the Earth unharmed."

"I'm not leaving without you! You have to come with me!"

"I can't," Shane said while avoiding Drew's sad eyes. "This is something I have to do."

"No," Drew protested.

"He's made up his mind," Amber snapped.

Suddenly, Amber closed her eyes and bright sparks began pulsating between her antennas. She pushed this energy towards Drew until it surrounded him completely.

"Goodbye, Drew," Shane said quietly as his friend disappeared.

"Don't be sad," Amber told Shane, once all the sparks had vanished. "We'll have so much fun together. What would you like to do first?"

"Nothing," Shane snapped.

"I'm sorry," Amber said. "But I'm doing what's best for me."

Shane said nothing as he walked back into the dark green and brown room and then opened the other door. Seeking solace, he stared into the vast, mesmerizing solar system until a beautiful red planet rotated by slowly.

"Huh?" Shane said as he noticed some strange things floating towards him. "Amber!" he screamed as they came into focus.

"What?" Amber asked, walking to Shane's side.

"Why are Mr. Ingles, Lance and Mr. Kannon floating through the solar system? You can't leave them like that – they'll die!"

Amber let out a high pitch laugh. "They'll be fine. I'll take them back to Earth in a few hours."

Shane closed the door. He couldn't stand to look at the frightening scene any longer.

"Don't look so scared," Amber teased as if everything was fine.

She really is evil, Shane thought, suddenly uncertain about his decision. Although he'd saved Earth from Amber's evilness, he was now at her mercy.

Back on Earth, Drew was telling his sobbing mother about where he'd been. As she held him in a tight embrace, he looked out the window.

I'll bring you back to Earth somehow, Drew silently vowed to Shane.

* * *

Jupiter's Revenge: An Amber Cook Sequel

"Now what?" Shane Radway muttered as he stared at his surroundings.

After being abducted by Amber – his so-called friend – and taken to Jupiter, Shane had wandered around the strange planet in a daze. He was surprised to find that Jupiter was a lot like Earth, with the exception of the solar system scenery, high-tech gadgets and the fact that everything looked metallic.

"Now I show you where I live," Amber answered, taking Shane by his arm and leading him towards a shiny but otherwise normal-looking bungalow.

"It's nice," Shane commented, not sure what else to say.

"Don't be silly," Amber said, knocking Shane with her hip.

Amber's playful knock caused Shane to lose his balance and land on a patch of cosmic green grass. He saw aliens looking at him as they walked by. However, they weren't pointing and laughing like he thought they would be. Instead, they cast him a sympathetic look.

Amber's high pitch laugh rang throughout the street. "You're such a wimp," she said mockingly, before offering her hand to him.

Ignoring her hand, Shane got onto his feet by himself. Even if he spent a hundred years trying to figure Amber out, he knew he'd never be successful.

To conceal the embarrassment of having her helpful gesture refused, Amber concentrated on opening the front door with the electricity from her antennas.

"These things have more than one use," Amber said as she pointed at her antennas.

Shane said nothing as he followed Amber inside. He immediately noticed that the interior of the house didn't look as normal as the exterior. The house was filled with expensive-looking devices that he'd never seen before.

"Do you want to meet my parents?" Amber asked excitedly. "For parents, they're actually kind of cool."

"No...no thanks," Shane replied, unable to keep his voice steady. He definitely didn't want to meet the couple who were responsible for raising such a crazy daughter.

"If you're going to be living here, you'll need to meet my parents eventually," Amber pointed out.

"Live here?"

"Duh!" Amber laughed, touching Shane's arm playfully. "Where else would you live?"

"Earth!" Shane exclaimed before he had time to think about what he was saying.

Amber's eyes clouded over. "You made your choice, so you better get used to it."

"I just want to get some air," Shane replied as he began to back out of the house.

"Okay. I'll show you more of Jupiter. It's so amazing here – I know you'll love it."

"I...I want to go for a walk by myself."

With a tense expression, Amber looked suspiciously at Shane. Suddenly, her face softened. "Okay, but be careful. Stay away from the objects you humans call cars. They move extra fast on Jupiter. You should also stay away from craters. They're very deep and dangerous. Aliens who fall into them are rarely ever seen again."

"Thanks," Shane said with a shiver as he proceeded out the door.

Once Shane was away from Amber, he felt a bit calmer. He planned on making an escape. He would go to a neighbor's house and ask for help. Maybe they would know how to get him back to Earth.

"Shane!" a familiar voice called.

Shane's heart sank as he turned around to see Amber hurrying towards him.

"On second thought, I think I'll join you," Amber said with a smile. "I wouldn't want you to get hurt."

I'll never escape, Shane thought with a heavy sigh.

As they walked, Shane admired the beautiful scenery. Stars twinkled brightly, and an occasional shooting star zoomed by. It was these stars, as well as strange-looking streetlamps, which provided Jupiter with light.

"Oh, no," Amber said suddenly. "It's the nerd squad."

Shane looked where Amber was pointing to see three teenage aliens. He instantly recognized them as the aliens Drew had befriended during his stay on Jupiter.

"Hi," Shane said as the aliens passed them.

The aliens, who had all been staring at their shoes, suddenly looked up.

"Hi," one of the aliens answered.

"Don't talk to them," Amber warned. "They're just nerds."

"Aren't you Drew's friend?" a different alien asked.

"Yeah," Shane said with a nod.

"We saw what you did for Drew," the third alien said. "That was very kind of you."

"Oh, please," Amber muttered. "You're such losers."

Although Amber's words were harsh, Shane noticed that she looked embarrassed and even a bit scared.

"Drew was a very smart human," one of the aliens said. "I'm Neil, by the way, and these are my friends, Sam and Chris."

"My name's Shane," he replied, shaking Neil's hand. "I'm surprised you aren't named Zip, Zap and Zop or something like that. Jupiter is actually a lot like Earth."

As Shane shook each of the alien's hands and talked with them, Amber's face turned a deep shade of red.

"Don't touch him!" Amber yelled, finally overcome with jealousy. "He's my friend – not yours."

Worried, Shane looked at Amber. *She's getting crazier by the minute.*

"What you've done to Shane is horrible," Neil said, staring angrily into Amber's eyes.

Sam and Chris muttered something to Neil and pulled him back from Amber.

"Oh, really?" Amber asked in a silky smooth voice.

"Yes," Neil replied harshly. "You still have the power to transport Shane back to Earth. Just let him go home."

"You shouldn't have won that contest," Sam said bravely, stepping beside Neil. "I can't wait until your powers fade away. They'll be gone soon and you'll be Miss Amber Nobody once again."

Amber looked absolutely furious. "The power is inside of me. I'll never lose it."

"You're fooling yourself," Chris said, also stepping forward.

"You know that the power is starting to fade already," Neil added.

"No, it's not!" Amber yelled as she jumped towards Neil.

Amber caught Neil off guard as she pushed him to the ground. Since the street was on a slight incline, Neil began rolling backwards, picking up momentum as he went. Unfortunately, he was heading straight towards a crater.

Shane, Chris and Sam ran frantically after Neil. Amber followed, obviously enjoying the ruckus she'd caused.

Neil screamed as he tumbled into the crater. Thinking fast, he grabbed onto the crater's edge. He held on, but only by the tips of his fingers.

"Help me!" Neil cried continuously.

Uncharacteristically, Shane backed away. Although he wanted to help, he was too afraid he'd fall over or be pushed by Amber. Instead, Shane watched as Sam and Chris began lifting up Neil. It took a while, but they finally managed to pull him to safety.

Amber laughed in an evil tone that Shane had never heard before. He looked once more at Neil's terrified face before running back to Amber's house.

"Wait, Shane!" Amber called as she ran after him. "What's wrong with you?" she asked, once they were both in her house.

Shane wanted to ask what was wrong with her, but he was too afraid to say such a thing. After all, Shane had seen what happened to Neil when he spoke his mind.

"I know what's wrong," Amber said quietly. "You think I was trying to kill Neil. I know it must have been scary for you, but he was in no danger. That's how we play on Jupiter."

Shane looked at Amber. He hadn't believed a word she'd said.

"Do you want some crackers and moon cheese?" Amber asked as she led him into the kitchen.

"No, thanks," Shane replied with a gulp. For some reason, he had no appetite.

* * *

Back on Earth, Drew stood at the scene of the crime. He was in the exact spot where Amber had generated that terrifying electrical field between her antennas and then zapped him to Jupiter.

Perhaps there's a portal which leads to Jupiter, and electricity is the key to its activation, Drew thought, narrowing his eyes as if challenging an unseen beast.

For days, Drew had been building a machine that generated a large amount of electrical power. It worked by collecting solar power and then storing it in two microchips. Now, he was finally ready to test his invention.

With a deep breath, Drew positioned his machine on the pavement and then turned it on. He stood back and watched as the machine created a small field of electricity. As the electrical field grew bigger, Drew threw a small metal ball into it. He watched as the ball shook harshly. Suddenly, the electrical field disappeared, and the ball melted into a silver patch on the pavement.

Drew sighed. He'd hoped the electrical field would work like the power of Amber's antennas and send him to Jupiter. When in Jupiter, he would rescue Shane. However, his plan had failed and he was out of ideas – not to mention money.

Drew picked up his machine and headed to his house. He was back at square one – trying to figure out a plan to get Shane home safely.

* * *

"Do you want to see what I brought back from Earth?" Amber asked, jumping up from the kitchen table.

Shane put down the crackers and moon cheese, which Amber had insisted he eat, and followed her through the house.

"This is my room," Amber said proudly as she hurried inside.

Shane stopped at her bedroom door and looked in. Her room was strewn with clothing, make-up and knick-knacks. Even her walls were covered with numerous posters of rock stars. These rock stars looked very much like Earth celebrities; the only difference was their green antennas.

"You can come in," Amber said with a laugh as she reached for something under her bed.

Cautiously, Shane proceeded into Amber's bedroom.

"Here they are!" Amber said happily while pulling out a large jar.

Shane looked at the jar closely. He saw nothing but blackness. "What's in there?"

"Earth ants," Amber replied with an evil smile. "I want to educate my fellow Jupiter residents about creatures from Earth."

"I don't think that's a good idea," Shane interjected. "You should never introduce a species into a new environment without applying controls first."

"You're starting to sound like Drew," Amber said, rolling her eyes. "That's an insult, by the way."

Shane felt his blood boil. He hated it when anyone made fun of Drew. "Do whatever you want," he finally snapped.

"I like that attitude," Amber said before hurrying to leave her house.

Not wanting to stay in the Cook's house alone, Shane followed Amber. When he caught up to her, he saw her pouring small amounts of the Earth ants through windows. Amber moved from house to house, releasing the ants evenly into the residences.

"What are you doing?" Shane cried.

"Having fun," Amber replied as she moved on to a new house and poured the remainder of the ants through the window.

"I really don't think you should've done that," Shane began to say. However, he was interrupted by screaming.

A few seconds later, Neil came running out of the house. Ants were crawling all over him as he jumped up and down.

"It's okay," Shane assured Neil.

"I...I was just sitting under my window reading a book when these horrible things came hurtling towards me. What are they?"

"They're ants from Earth," Shane explained. "Although they're annoying, this kind of ant won't hurt you."

"How did they get into my house?" Neil cried, still wiping his body even though all the ants were gone.

Shane opened his mouth to answer but was interrupted once again. This time the interruption came from the house beside Neil's. A young female alien, who was acting like Neil had, came running out of her house. One by one, aliens emerged from their houses, all jumping up and down while yelling in terror. During all the hysteria, Amber's laugh could be heard loud and clear.

Neil turned and glared at Amber. "What's wrong with you?"

Sam and Chris, who had just run out of their houses as well, joined Neil. They all stood facing Amber with their arms crossed and bearing angry expressions.

"I'm just having fun," Amber said with a wide smile.

"This isn't funny," Neil's neighbor said, joining the growing group of residents who were facing Amber.

"Lighten up," Amber teased.

"My whole house is crawling with these things," an older male alien complained. "It'll take hours to get them out of there."

"Then you better get started," Amber said with another high pitch laugh as she grabbed Shane and pulled him back to her house.

For over two hours, Neil, along with the help of Sam and Chris, had been trapping the horrible Earth ants in his house.

"I hate Amber," Neil muttered as he caught the remaining ants in a jar.

"That makes two of us," Sam agreed.

"Make that three," Chris chimed in.

"She's really getting out of control," Neil commented.

"I know," Sam agreed once again. "First she kidnaps Shane, then she almost kills Neil, and now she's infested Jupiter with ants from Earth."

"She's got to be dealt with," Chris said. Noticing Neil and Sam's curious expressions, he continued. "I've been thinking about how we can get rid of her, and I've come up with a good plan. Amber only has five hours and thirty six minutes left of her transportation power. We need to convince Shane to hide from Amber. Then we tell her that he's escaped back to Earth. We'll do all of this in such a precise manner that Amber will transport herself back to Earth in search of Shane, just minutes before her transportation power runs out."

"So, Amber won't be able to get back to Jupiter!" Sam concluded happily. "That's a great plan, Chris."

"It is a good plan," Neil agreed, "but what will the king and queen of Jupiter say when Amber never returns home? They will surely bring her back by their own powers."

"I've thought about that already," Chris replied, somewhat defensively. "We'll tell them that Amber liked Earth better than Jupiter, and she's decided to live there forever."

"Besides," Sam added quickly, "the king and queen don't like her any more than we do. Do you remember the time she broke the ring of Jupiter by intentionally skating on it with the wrong type of footwear? It took the king and queen a year to fix it. If you add that incident to all the others, I can confidently conclude that Amber Cook is not a well-liked person."

"There's one other problem," Neil noted, after listening to Sam's reasoning. "Shane will be stuck on Jupiter forever. The plan really isn't fair to him."

"As far as I see it," Chris argued, "it's a better fate than the one he has right now."

Sam and Chris looked expectantly at Neil.

"Alright," Neil said finally. "We'll carry out Chris' plan, but with one modification. We'll keep Shane hidden nearby, so he can jump into Amber's electricity as she transports herself to Earth."

"That sounds very reasonable," Chris said, nodding his head. "That way Shane can go home and we'll be permanently free of the awful Amber Cook!"

"Don't you have any soda?" Shane asked, looking into the Cook's high-tech refrigerator. He was trying to keep calm and forget about the awful trick Amber had played with the Earth ants.

"No. My parents won't let me drink soda. They say it makes me too hyper."

"Could I have some money to buy one?" Shane asked with wide, innocent eyes.

"Sure. I'll take you to the grocery store."

Shane rolled his eyes like Amber always did. "I can walk by myself."

Amber looked at Shane for a moment and then dug into her pocket to pull out a fancy-looking coin. "Okay. Do you remember where the grocery store is?"

"Yeah."

Amber smiled as she tossed the coin to him. "I charge interest."

"Thanks," Shane said before hurrying out of the house and down the street. He didn't really want a soda; he just needed to get away from Amber.

"Shane!" someone whispered loudly. "Hey, Shane! Over here!"

Shane looked around but couldn't see anyone.

"Over here, Shane!" the voice said again.

Shane followed the voice until he came to a big cosmic green bush. He looked behind it to find Neil, Sam and Chris standing there suspiciously.

"Follow us," Neil said quietly.

Shane gulped. He didn't know if he should trust them. After all, he'd been with Amber when she almost pushed Neil into the crater, and even when she released the ants. Maybe they thought he'd been a part of Amber's evil plans.

"You don't have to be afraid of us," Neil said, sensing Shane's uncertainty.

Ignoring his instincts, Shane followed Sam, Neil and Chris as they maneuvered discreetly between houses. They finally stopped when Amber's house was in the distance.

"What do you want?" Shane asked nervously.

"We feel bad for you," Sam blurted out.

"Why do you feel bad for me?" Shane asked with a racing heart, fearing that they were going to hurt him.

"What Sam means is that we want to help you," Neil explained. "We'll help you get back to Earth."

"Why would you help me?"

"We feel sorry for you and want to help you," Chris said in an unconvincing manner.

"I heard you the first time," Shane snapped. He felt ashamed after he'd spoken. "Sorry. I've been spending so much time with Amber that her rudeness is starting to rub off on me."

"That's okay," Neil said with a friendly smile. "You actually survived longer than anyone thought you would."

"I've figured out a plan to get you back to Earth," Chris hurried to explain. "If we hide you from Amber and then tell her that you've escaped to Earth, she'll transport herself to Earth in search of you. When she has the electricity surrounding her, you'll jump in and be transported back to Earth as well."

"I don't like this plan," Shane admitted. "Amber will be furious and just bring me back to Jupiter anyway."

"But that's the brilliance of the plan," Chris argued. "She won't be able to bring you back because her power of transportation will soon be ending. The contest is almost over and when it ends, Amber will be zapped back to Jupiter. You'll be home, safe and sound, and Amber will never be able to visit Earth again."

"Do you really think your plan will work?" Shane asked skeptically.

Chris nodded enthusiastically. "It'll work perfectly. All you have to do is hide and jump into the electrical field. We'll deal with the rest."

"Okay, I guess it's worth a try."

"Good," Sam piped in with a smile. "I'll hide you in my house and then we'll lure Amber there."

As Shane followed Sam to his house, he prayed that he'd made the right decision.

Inside her house, Amber stormed back and forth. Shane had been gone for hours. Since the grocery store was only a five minute walk from her house, she was sure he hadn't got lost. Instead, Amber was convinced that he'd run away. This thought made her furious. She didn't understand why Shane would do such a thing. After all, she had been nicer to Shane than anyone else she'd ever met.

Amber was just about to storm out of her house in search of Shane when the telephone rang. "What do you want?" she snapped into the phone.

"Amber, it's Sam," Sam said breathlessly. "I just saw Shane go through an electrical field. He's gone back to Earth!"

"But that's impossible!"

"That's what I thought," Sam agreed, "but he was standing in my house when all of a sudden, he disappeared into an electrical field. Before he disappeared, Shane said he'd found a device that could take him back to Earth."

"Why was he in your house?" Amber asked suspiciously.

"He wanted to talk," Sam replied. "He said horrible things about you, but I defended you, Amber."

Amber's blood boiled. She was hurt and angry that Shane would say anything bad about her. "I'm coming over right now," she said, before slamming the phone down.

"Did you really have to say all that?" Shane cried, once Sam had hung up the phone.

"I needed to get her angry enough to come over here," Sam explained.

"She'll kill me!"

"Only if she catches you," Neil pointed out while pulling Shane behind a nearby couch.

Chris joined them behind the couch and then asked, "Do you remember the plan?"

"Of course," Shane answered with determination.

A few moments later, a loud pounding sounded upon the door. As soon as Sam opened it, Amber rushed in.

"Where's the device Shane used to travel back to Earth?" Amber demanded.

"He...he took it with him," Sam stuttered.

Shane's heart raced. He was suddenly terrified that the plan wouldn't work. After all, Sam did sound pretty nervous.

"I'm going to bring him back," Amber said fiercely.

As Amber stood in the middle of Sam's room, her antennas rose up from her head and an electrical field twirled around her. The electrical field wasn't as strong as it had been. A look of concern washed over Amber's face. However, within a few minutes, the electrical field was at its full power once again.

"Now," Chris whispered to Shane as Amber began to disappear.

Shane jumped out from behind the couch and into the electrical field with Amber. He felt the familiar cold sensation as he was engulfed in the electrical waves and transported back to Earth.

Sam, Neil and Chris stood around the fading electrical field. They'd heard a surprised cry come from Amber when Shane had entered the electrical field.

"Do you think we did the right thing?" Neil asked his friends as he watched the electrical field disappear completely.

Neither Sam nor Chris answered Neil's question. Instead, they smiled widely.

* * *

Back on Earth, Drew looked up at the night sky. His eyes were fixed on the bright planet that was Jupiter.

"Shane," Drew said sadly, "I've spent every waking moment trying to come up with a plan to save you, but I've failed. None of my ideas have worked." He stopped talking to choke back a sob. "The police have started a huge campaign to find Amber, but they'll never find her."

Drew stood at his bedroom window and placed his hand against the cool glass. "I guess this is goodbye, my friend."

"Shane, I'm going to kill you!" Amber screamed as they tossed and turned in the electrical field.

When they landed on the ground, Shane began to run. Although he was happy to be back on Earth, he knew he didn't have time to rejoice; he had to get away from Amber.

"Come back here!" Amber yelled, her loud voice carrying throughout the dark street.

"No chance!" Shane yelled back, looking over his shoulder.

Suddenly, Shane fell to the ground. He'd tripped over a skateboard that someone had left on the sidewalk. Shane looked up in fear as Amber stood over him and then grabbed him by his t-shirt.

As Drew continued to look out the window, his eyes fell upon two people who were running. He watched as one of them fell to the ground.

"Shane? Amber?" Drew exclaimed, before running through his bedroom and down the stairs. He rushed out into the cool night air just in time to see Amber grabbing Shane's t-shirt.

"Why did you run away?" Amber asked, more upset than angry. Neither she nor Shane had seen Drew yet.

Shane looked at Amber in surprise. He was shocked to hear her tone of voice. He had thought Amber would be pulverizing him by now.

"It was all Neil, Sam and Chris' idea," Shane explained. "They said this was the only way to get back to Earth."

"I'll deal with them when we get back to Jupiter," Amber said harshly, revealing her antennas and creating the electrical field.

Shane tried, unsuccessfully, to struggle out of Amber's grasp.

"No!" Drew cried, finally stepping into the action. "Let Shane go!"

"Drew!" Shane cried in surprise.

"Stand back, Drew," Amber said. "This is between Shane and me."

The electrical field around Amber's antennas weakened. Suddenly, the electrical field burnt out completely.

"Oh, no!" Amber cried with terror.

Catching Amber off guard, Shane tore himself from her grasp and then ran towards Drew.

"Chris said your power of transportation would run out soon. I guess he was right!" Shane shouted at Amber. "Just go back to Jupiter. I never want to see you again!"

Amber's eyes were filled with terror. "You idiot! Now that my power of transportation is gone, I can't get back to Jupiter!"

"But...but Neil, Sam and Chris said you'd be zapped back to Jupiter."

"They lied," Amber snapped. "They knew I wouldn't be able to return to Jupiter once my powers died. I bet they've even lied to my parents as well as the king and queen of Jupiter – no one will ever come looking for me!"

"What does this mean?" Shane asked Amber with wide, frightened eyes.

"It means that we've both been fooled," Amber complained. "I'll have to spend the rest of my life on Earth." She shook her head in disappointment and then began to walk away. "I'll be seeing you two again," she added sinisterly as she disappeared down the street.

"I'm glad you're home," Drew said, while slapping him affectionately on the shoulder.

"That makes two of us," Shane replied. "But what about Amber? We'll never get rid of her!"

"Oh, I think we will," Drew said with a secret smile.

"What do you mean?"

Drew remained smiling as he led Shane to a nearby tree. "Do you see that sign?" he asked, pointing to a poster that was stapled to the tree.

A smile slowly spread over Shane's face as he looked at the official police poster which had a photograph of Amber on it. Underneath her picture was the word, *Wanted*.

"Drew, my friend," Shane said as he approached a payphone and began to call the police, "I think our problem is over."

* * *

Revenge Of The Fortune-Teller

An early morning fog surrounded seventeen-year-old Sage Michaels as she hurried towards the carnival. Getting closer, she looked up to see the rides, which loomed high in the sky and seemingly disappeared into the low grey clouds. She could even hear an echo of hammers and saws being used by rushed workmen. Excited, Sage approached the front gates.

"Hello," Sage greeted a scruffy-looking security guard who manned the gates.

"The carnival is closed," the security guard snapped, hardly looking up as he texted on his cellphone.

Sage was deeply annoyed by his remark. The Ringo Carnival had come every year to her town of Oakwood Valley since she was five years old. As a regular visitor, she knew they opened on the first day of summer and closed after the Labor Day weekend.

"Cat got your tongue, kid?" the security guard snickered, finally putting away his cellphone to pay attention to her.

"I'm not here as a customer," Sage replied as calmly as she could. "I'm looking for the manager."

"What do you want him for?"

"If you must know, I'm applying for a job."

The security guard looked Sage up and down. "Aren't you a bit young to be employed?" he asked mockingly.

"No," she replied sharply.

"Fine," the security guard said with a heavy sigh, obviously annoyed that he had to leave his post. "I'll take you to Ringo."

"Thanks," Sage responded in an ungrateful tone. She sincerely hoped that the rest of the staff wouldn't be as unpleasant as this man.

The security guard hurried throughout the carnival. Sage was forced to keep up, even though she yearned to stop and watch the colorful tents being assembled.

"Ringo!" the security guard called as he stopped outside a small white trailer. "Hey, Ringo!" he continued to call, while knocking upon the door.

"What do you want?" Ringo snapped after he'd flung open the trailer door.

"This girl is looking for a job," the security guard replied, shoving his thumb towards Sage's face. Then, without even saying goodbye, he hurried away.

"So, you're looking for a job, huh?" Ringo inquired.

"Yes," Sage replied, taken aback once again by the unfriendliness of the carnival workers.

As Sage stared at Ringo, she was surprised by his appearance. He had long grey hair which was tied in a ponytail. Long stubble grew on his face, as if he was trying to decide whether or not to grow a beard. Ringo was also dressed in an untidy manner. His black t-shirt, which looked like it had been bleached in several spots, contained many moth holes. Even his jean shorts were a mess; it looked like they'd unraveled by a foot.

"Well, there are no jobs," Ringo snapped.

"But you advertised for help in the newspaper," Sage protested.

"That was before we needed a different type of help," Ringo said, less harsh this time.

"I don't understand."

"My carnival is falling apart!" Ringo exclaimed unexpectedly, while throwing his hands in the air. "I lost the sponsorship from Family Value Superstore – the company that provided me with the most money."

"Everything seems to be coming along normally," Sage replied, glancing at the several tents which surrounded them. "I should know," she added. "I've been coming here for twelve years."

"Thanks, kid," Ringo said, obviously warming up to Sage. "But I'm afraid there are no jobs available. We've had to make a lot of cutbacks."

Sage was just about to express her disappointment and say goodbye when a commotion nearby made her and Ringo spin around. They stared in shock as a woman, who wore a flowing purple dress and a ton of chunky gold jewelry, ushered a guilty-looking boy out of a tent.

"Get out of my lair, and never come back!" the woman yelled.

"I'm sorry," the boy, who looked as if he was fifteen, said. "I know I shouldn't have done it. Can't you just forgive me?"

"Madame Zerona cannot forgive those who steal from her!" the woman cried, referring to herself in the third person.

The boy's apologetic demeanor faded quickly. "Fine," he snapped. "See if I care. I can get another job where my employer *isn't* a fake!"

Madame Zerona looked wild with anger. "You'll be sorry!" she yelled, as the boy ran towards the carnival's exit.

Ringo turned his attention back to Sage. "Perhaps we have a job opportunity after all."

"Is Madame Zerona a fortune-teller?" Sage asked with wide eyes.

Ringo nodded. "Why don't you see if she's willing to hire you?"

Sage wasn't sure if now was a good time to approach Madame Zerona. She had looked pretty angry. However, Sage's need for money clouded her judgment. She would be going to college next year, and although her parents would cover the tuition, it was her responsibility to pay for books and supplies.

"I'll talk to her right now," Sage replied, while watching Madame Zerona dash back into her yellow and purple tent. "Don't worry about the carnival," she added, turning around to face Ringo once again. "Business will be better than ever!"

Ringo cast Sage a doubtful smile before entering his trailer and closing the door.

Taking a deep breath, Sage stepped into the tent marked, *Madame Zerona's Lair*. She would've knocked on the door first, but there was none. In fact, the whole lair seemed to be nothing more than a few large sheets of fabric and some poles to make the frame. It appeared very flimsy and blew harshly with the winds.

"Hello!" Sage called. "Madame Zerona, are you in here? My name is Sage Michaels. I'm looking for a job, and Ringo said you might need some help." The deeper she went into the lair, the darker it became. "Hello!" she called again.

A bright light, followed by the appearance of Madame Zerona startled Sage.

"I've been waiting for you," Madame Zerona said in a wispy voice as she pointed her long, skinny finger towards Sage's chest. "You're just what I want."

"I...I am?" Sage stammered.

"Oh, yes," Madame Zerona said while circling Sage.

Sage let out a small gasp as a multi-colored light filled the tent, making everything inside suddenly visible. There were several shelves jam-packed with odd knick-knacks and glass jars filled with unidentifiable ingredients. Sage's attention was particularly drawn to the middle of the tent where a large crystal ball sat upon a cloth-covered table.

"This place is amazing," Sage muttered in awe.

"Thanks," Madame Zerona said, quickly changing her serious tone into a happy one. "Um, I mean thank you," she repeated in her signature wispy voice. "I have a feeling you're in need of work."

"Yes, I am," Sage confirmed.

Madame Zerona's long purple dress swirled magnificently as she hurried to the cloth-covered table and sat down in one of the chairs. She moved her ring-adorned fingers over the crystal ball. "I see," she began slowly, "I see..." Madame Zerona suddenly stopped what she was doing to ask, "Can you look away for a moment?"

Sage turned her head away, but from the corner of her eye she saw Madame Zerona lift up the crystal ball and turn on a switch.

"You may turn around now," Madame Zerona said in a mysterious manner. She shifted her attention towards the crystal ball which now contained a purple fog. "I see you and I having a wonderful relationship," she predicted.

"I'm sure we will," Sage hurried to agree.

"Do you know anything about magic?" Madame Zerona asked, casting a hopeful glance at Sage.

"A little. I've had my palm read before, and I've even been hypnotized. I'm a fast learner and would be more than willing to educate myself on the finer points of magic."

"The job is yours," Madame Zerona told Sage. "But I better not catch you stealing. You saw what happened to the last assistant who tried to steal from me."

"I'd never do that."

"You better not," Madame Zerona threatened in a low tone. "Remember, I see everything."

It's a good thing I don't steal, Sage thought while smiling pleasantly at Madame Zerona, *because I'm no more of a thief than she is a real fortune-teller.*

* * *

The next morning, Sage woke up early, ate breakfast and then hurried to the carnival. She was meant to meet Madame Zerona at 9 a.m. for training, but she was so excited to start her first day of work that she arrived at 8:30.

Ever since she was a little girl, Sage had loved The Ringo Carnival. She adored the midway games and the cheap prizes they offered. However, it was the rides that took her breath away. Her favorite had always been *The Adventure Zone.* This attraction was a large obstacle course filled with moving floors, trick mirrors, and tons of plastic balls. This wasn't just a regular obstacle course though. It was actually a game where the participants searched for hidden gems. Although these gems were nothing more than plastic imitations, Sage felt a rush every time she found one.

As Sage entered the front gates, she smiled widely and strutted past the security guard.

"Did you get a job then?" the security guard inquired.

"Of course," Sage replied in a superior manner as she walked away with her head held high. Although she wasn't usually rude to people, she was willing to make an exception for him.

Sage looked around in interest as she walked through the midway. Most of the rides and game booths had already been assembled. All that was left to do was plug in the machines and get the prizes in order. Even though the rides and booths looked great, the owners were in a frenzy trying to get everything perfect for the carnival's grand opening tomorrow.

"Madame Zerona!" Sage called before entering the fortune-telling tent.

Sage let out a gasp as soon as she stepped inside. There, in the middle of the brightly lit tent, was Madame Zerona. The crystal ball was upside-down as she tried to fix the base with a screwdriver. Two AA batteries lay on the table beside her. Madame Zerona's face went a deep shade of red as she tried to cover the crystal ball and batteries under the table cloth. Her attempt to conceal her fraud was done in vain as a battery rolled off the table and onto the floor.

"Sage, I...I wasn't expecting you so soon," Madame Zerona stammered.

Obviously, Sage thought as she picked up the battery and handed it to Madame Zerona. "I'm a very punctual person," she finally replied.

"We should get started," Madame Zerona said, while trying to casually put the crystal ball back into one piece. "I have a lot to teach you. I need my assistant to control the lighting and fog within the tent. Do you have any experience with electronics?"

"I've been a part of my high school's AV club for three years – it's my passion," Sage replied with rising excitement.

"Excellent!"

Madame Zerona spent the next few hours teaching Sage how to operate the lighting and fog machines, along with other devices which were either cool or creepy. By the end of the day, Sage had mastered the art of phony fortune-telling props.

I'll remember this job for the rest of my life, Sage thought, ecstatic that she was earning money while honing her technical skills.

Sage's thoughts were correct. No matter how much she'd want to forget this job, she would remember it forever.

* * *

People were already lining up for the carnival's opening day when Sage arrived at work. Feeling like an important person, she passed the bystanders and hurried through the front gates.

The carnival had come to life; music blared throughout the area and multi-colored lights flashed on the rides.

Sage felt a rush of excitement as she headed towards the fortune-telling tent. It was the same feeling she always got when she went to the carnival.

"Hurry up and get dressed," Madame Zerona commanded as soon as Sage entered the tent. "I don't want anyone to see you without your costume."

Sage suppressed the urge to roll her eyes. *Did Madame Zerona really expect me to walk to the carnival in my costume?* she thought as she pulled a long purple dress out of her backpack.

In a private section of the tent, Sage put on the dress. It was shapeless and far too long; at least a foot of fabric trailed behind her. Next, Sage clipped three purple hair extensions onto her real hair. She smiled as she looked in the mirror. The contrast between her natural blonde hair and the purple extensions looked amazing.

"Are you ready?" Madame Zerona called to Sage.

"Almost," Sage replied, while pressing on fake nails and then gently applying fake eyelashes along her eyelids.

It was Sage's job to stand outside the tent and encourage potential customers to get their fortunes read. She also had to guide the customers inside and then disappear to operate the special effects machines. Although Sage hated deceiving people, she knew it was all just for fun.

"Are you ready yet?" Madame Zerona called to Sage in a much more frantic voice.

Sage finished applying purple eye shadow and then emerged from the back of the tent.

"Oh, you look wonderful!" Madame Zerona exclaimed. "Just like a real fortune-teller."

"Then I'm sure I can pass for a fortune-teller's assistant," Sage said with a laugh, before walking towards the tent's entrance.

Suddenly, Sage fell over the long hem of her dress. She landed on the ground with a sickening thud. At first she was surprised by the fall. However, in a few seconds she was laughing so hard that tears rolled down her face.

"I'm so clumsy," Sage admitted as a woman offered her a hand. After taking her hand and pulling herself up, she gasped to discover it wasn't Madame

Zerona who stood before her. Sage was deadly still as she stared at the woman.

The woman, who was short and somewhat plump, wore a black pleated dress that was adorned with embroidered yellow flowers. She was over accessorized with large hoop earrings and several beaded necklaces and bracelets; all her jewelry was black. From the deep wrinkles on her face to her long silver hair, Sage assumed she must be over a hundred years old.

"Who are you and what are you doing in my lair?" Madame Zerona demanded, after she'd hurried to Sage's side and seen the strange old woman who was dressed like a fortune-teller.

"I am Josephine," the woman answered angrily. "I am a real fortune-teller, and I have come to seek my revenge on those who falsely claim to have the powers which I possess."

Not the least bit frightened, Madame Zerona looked at Josephine as if she was insane.

Despite the chills which Josephine's presence caused, Sage couldn't help but see the irony in the situation. Madame Zerona was obviously not afraid of Josephine because she didn't believe that real fortune-tellers existed.

"Get out of my lair," Madame Zerona said in annoyance.

Josephine tilted her head backwards and laughed. "A lair?" she mocked, while walking around the tent. She lifted up a glass jar that was filled with green leaves and laughed again. "You call this a lair?" Josephine swept her hand over the numerous jars which sat on the shelves. "These are cooking herbs! Nothing more than what you'd find in the grocery section of Family Value Superstore."

"You can't prove that," Madame Zerona responded, trying to keep calm.

Although Josephine was two feet shorter than Madame Zerona, she approached her and then looked up to cast a challenging stare. "You are a fraud, Madame Zerona," Josephine said loud and clear.

"That's it!" Madame Zerona cried as her face went red with anger. "If you don't leave right now, I'll call security!"

"I'll leave now, but I shall be back," Josephine remarked, before disappearing through the tent's exit.

"What just happened?" Sage asked, while peeking outside the tent to see Josephine marching away. She immediately noticed that a small crowd had gathered, most likely to see what all the commotion was about.

Madame Zerona shook her head in confusion. "I have no clue," she replied honestly. "Somehow she knows who I am, but I've never seen her before."

* * *

The next day, Sage arrived very early at the fortune-telling tent because Madame Zerona had insisted they practice their routine more thoroughly. She prayed that today would go much smoother than yesterday.

Everything had gone downhill after Josephine's appearance. Although Madame Zerona and Josephine's fight had created a lot of attention, causing many people to come for a fortune reading, the sudden rush of customers overwhelmed the already stressed Madame Zerona and Sage. This stress was visible through their work as Sage accidentally sprayed a boy with purple fog and Madame Zerona unwittingly told a girl, who'd come for a palm reading, that she would have a short lifespan.

Sage and Madame Zerona spent the next two hours rehearsing vigorously. When the carnival opened, Sage took her post outside the tent. Their first customer didn't arrive until fifteen minutes later.

"Welcome to Madame Zerona's lair of fortune-telling," Sage greeted the teenage girl in a low voice. "Follow me to discover her wonderful powers."

Sage threw the entrance to the tent open. Although she was meant to lead the customer inside, she held back to stare at a woman in the crowd.

"Should I go inside?" the girl inquired, causing Sage to return her attention to the job.

"Um, no, follow me," Sage muttered, leading the girl into the lair and then disappearing behind a curtain to control the special effects.

As she hit the button to release the purple fog, Sage wished that Madame Zerona would hurry up and finish the girl's fortune reading. She thought it was very important to tell her that she'd seen Josephine in the crowd.

Sage listened carefully, synchronizing her actions to Madame Zerona's words. Whenever Madame Zerona made a dramatic prediction, Sage would dim the lights and release the multi-colored fog. It was a delicate art of balance and timing, and Sage knew she was doing great.

Suddenly, Sage smelled something unusual – it was smoke! Her eyes widened as she saw an orange flame rise up the side of the tent.

"Madame Zerona!" Sage yelled, running out from her hiding place. "The tent is on fire!"

Madame Zerona and the girl looked startled by Sage's warning. Suddenly, the girl screamed as she saw the flames creep along the tent behind Madame Zerona.

Following the girl's gaze, Madame Zerona turned around. Finally seeing the fire, she jumped up from her chair. "My beautiful lair!" she shrieked in horror.

By now, the flames had crept half way up the tent and were spreading quickly.

"We have to get out of here!" the girl cried.

Sage turned her eyes away from the dancing flames and ran to the exit, followed by the girl and Madame Zerona. Once they were outside, they stared at the burning tent.

"I'll get help!" Sage cried, before maneuvering through the onlookers and racing towards the emergency station. She knew the tent would burn very quickly and that its only chance of salvation would come from quick action.

"There's a fire at the fortune-telling tent!" Sage yelled, when she finally reached the emergency station.

The two firefighters, who had been sitting peacefully at their desks a moment ago, sprang into action. Sage and the firefighters hurried into the small fire truck that was parked outside and then sped to Madame Zerona's tent.

When they arrived, it was already too late. All that was left of the tent were a few base poles, ashes and black smoke.

Sage tried to comfort a hysterical Madame Zerona, who was weeping on the ground, but she was inconsolable.

As the firefighters drenched what was left of the tent, Sage could see her summer of fun and money go up in smoke. Overcome with fury, she yelled, "Josephine did it!"

* * *

That night, Sage tossed and turned in a sleepless state. Images from the horrible day she'd just had circulated in her mind and refused to go away.

After proclaiming Josephine's guilt, Sage had to back up her accusation with proof. Unfortunately, she didn't have any incriminating evidence. Madame Zerona didn't need any proof though. She was positive that Josephine had started the fire. If the police wouldn't bring Josephine to justice, then Madame Zerona had promised to do so herself.

During the early hours of the morning, Sage finally fell into a restless sleep that was filled with nightmares about carnivals, fortune-tellers and fires.

"Sage, wake up."

Sage moaned in response.

"Wake up," the voice came again. "There's someone on the phone for you."

Sage finally awoke to see her mother, Mrs. Michaels, standing over her with a cordless telephone in her hand.

"Get out of bed," Mrs. Michaels scolded. "I have to go to work."

Sage groaned as she reached for the phone. "Hello?" she answered, while watching her mother leave the room.

"Sage," a woman said abruptly. "You must come to my lair at once."

"Lair?" Sage repeated. "Is this Madame Zerona?"

"Of course not. It is I, Josephine."

Sage gasped. "How did you get my phone number?"

"I know everything. I know your phone number, where you live and what you're doing right now."

"Then what am I doing now?" Sage challenged.

"The obvious answer? You're talking on the phone. However, the answer you're looking for is that you're biting your lip and clutching a hideous-looking teddy bear."

Sage stopped biting her lip and let go of Snuggly, the teddy bear she'd had for over a decade. "What do you want?" she demanded with a racing heart.

"I want you to come to my lair."

"Why would I do that?" Sage cried. "I hardly know you, and what I do know scares me!"

"You'll come to my lair because you're a loyal assistant who would hate to see her employer get hurt," Josephine said in a leading tone of voice.

"What...what do you mean?" Sage stuttered.

"Madame Zerona is at my lair and she's all tied up."

"Why are you doing this?" Sage screamed. Not waiting for an answer, she hung up the phone and then threw it on the floor. She didn't care if she broke her phone; all she cared about was putting distance between Josephine and herself.

"I know you're there," Josephine's voice echoed throughout the room. "If you don't come to me, I'll come to you."

"No!" Sage screamed as she kicked the phone hard against the wall.

Ding dong. Ding dong. Ding dong.

The sound of the ringing doorbell made Sage freeze in terror. *Josephine is crazy*, she realized, while opening her closet and rummaging through it.

Ding dong. Ding dong. Ding dong.

She followed me home from the carnival and has been spying on me, Sage thought. *That's how she knew what I was doing while talking to her on the phone.*

Sage shuddered with fear as she finally grasped the object she'd been seeking.

Ding dong. Ding dong. Ding dong.

Sage breathed heavily as she held the baseball bat tightly and then proceeded towards the front door. Through the glass panels, she could see the silhouette of a short woman.

Ding dong. Ding dong. Ding dong.

No one in their right mind would ring a doorbell that many times, Sage thought as she leaned closer to the door in order to see through the peephole. She was almost there when a pair of hands crashed through the glass and grabbed her. Sage didn't even have a chance to scream.

Sage's head pounded and her whole body ached. Her eyes fluttered open to reveal that she was no longer in her house. She was in a dark room that was lit with a few candles. Other than that, Sage could see nothing. She groaned in pain, frustration and confusion.

"Are you okay, Sage?" someone whispered.

Sage jumped at the sudden noise. She tried to move but soon realized that she was tied to a chair.

"Who's there?" Sage demanded.

"Shhh...Are you okay?" the voice came again.

"Of course not! I've been kidnapped! Who am I talking to?"

"It's Madame Zerona. I'm so sorry for getting you into this mess."

Sage's heart raced as she processed Madame Zerona's words. "Exactly what type of mess are we in?"

"I…I don't really know," Madame Zerona confessed.

"Of course Madame Zerona doesn't know," someone suddenly said in a creepy manner. "She's a fraud."

Sage let out a startled cry and then watched with wide eyes as a cloud of bright smoke appeared, bringing Josephine with it. It was like she'd materialized from the smoke.

"Hello, Sage," Josephine greeted with an evil smile, as the smoke continued to circle her.

"Why are you doing this?" Sage cried in frustration as tears brimmed her eyes.

"Because people like Madame Zerona have ruined my good name for too long. I warned you, but you wouldn't stop pretending."

"You've taken this too far," Madame Zerona said as firmly as she could. However, her voice quivered a little when she added, "If you let us go now, we can forget that this ever happened."

Angrily, Josephine raised her hands in the air. Bright smoke poured from her fingertips and filled the room. The smoke lingered near the floor, revealing that they were in a small room filled with odd talismans and bundles of dried flora.

"Nice special effects," Madame Zerona sneered.

"Stop it, Madame Zerona," Sage begged. "Josephine's the real thing – show her some respect."

Sage wasn't sure if she believed Josephine was a real fortune-teller. What she did know, however, was that Josephine had a very unstable personality. The last thing she wanted to do was offend her.

"I thought you were in the AV club at school," Madame Zerona retorted. "Surely you know that Josephine's smoke is just a prop."

"Be quiet," Sage muttered to Madame Zerona.

"You should listen to her," Josephine advised Madame Zerona. "She has a lot more sense than you."

"Let us go," Madame Zerona demanded.

"I will not let you go," Josephine said as she stepped closer to Madame Zerona. "At least not until you sign this contract." She snapped her fingers, causing a piece of paper to suddenly appear.

"A...a contract for what?" Madame Zerona asked shakily, unable to keep calm any longer.

"The contract states that you are not a real fortune-teller. It also guarantees that you'll never work as one again. What do you say, Madame Zerona? Will you finally admit your lies and promise to never impersonate a true fortune-teller again?"

"If I sign this contract, you'll let me go?" Madame Zerona asked skeptically.

"Yes, but it can't be taken lightly. If you sign this contract and then infringe upon it, I'll know instantly. I assure you that the consequences of such a breach are rather unpleasant."

"I believe you're a real fortune-teller," Madame Zerona said, almost in tears. "I'll sign the contract. Just please don't hurt me."

As Josephine snapped her fingers, the ropes which bound Madame Zerona to the chair fell on the floor.

Shakily, Madame Zerona signed the contract.

"You've made the right choice," Josephine said, right before the entire room filled with a dense black smoke.

"What's happening?" Sage yelled dizzily. "Madame Zerona, where are you?"

"She's been released," Josephine replied through the darkness.

When the black smoke began to disperse, Sage realized that she and Josephine were alone in a magical-looking forest.

"What is this place?" Sage cried as she looked at her surroundings.

Everything seemed surreal. The trees were enormous and the grass was unnaturally long and thick. Even the sky looked odd, as if it could thunder at any moment, despite the presence of a bright blood orange sun.

Josephine took Sage's hands in her own, causing Sage to finally realize that she had also been released from the ropes.

"This is our land, my dear. Although we've now integrated with regular society, this will always be our home." Noting Sage's confused expression, Josephine continued. "I've been traveling the world for the last five years, revealing all the fake fortune-tellers for what they really are. My traveling has come to an end, and my first purpose has been fulfilled. Now, I want to re-establish the reputation of my people, and I could use an apprentice. You have what I'm looking for, Sage. You're a real fortune-teller with unlimited powers."

"I'm not a fortune-teller, and I don't possess any special skills!" Sage exclaimed.

"Yes, you do. You just don't know it because they haven't been nurtured. I can help bring your powers to the surface."

"If I do have these powers, I'm not sure I want to use them," Sage admitted slowly.

"You must!" Josephine exclaimed, while tightening her grip on Sage. "When our ancestors found a way out of this land, the world suddenly became limitless. It also became a lot more dangerous. If we are to let people know that fortune-tellers truly exist, we must stick together."

"And if I refuse?" Sage asked boldly.

"Then you'll share the same fate as the fake fortune-tellers who wouldn't sign the contract."

"I don't believe you!" Sage shouted as she forced her hands from Josephine's grasp and then ran away.

Shocked, Josephine stumbled backwards. However, she quickly recovered and began to chase after Sage.

Sage hurried through the tall grass, wincing as it scratched her.

"Get back here!" Josephine shrieked.

No way! Sage thought as she increased her speed.

Sage had been running for several minutes now. Her lungs ached and a sharp pain kept stabbing at her side. She slowed down and turned around. Josephine was nowhere in sight.

"Yes! I've lost her!" Sage said happily, while preparing to sit on an unusually large fallen tree branch.

"You may have lost me," a creepy voice taunted, "but I've certainly found you."

Sage spun around and then gasped upon seeing Josephine. "How did you find me?"

"The power of a fortune-teller goes well beyond anything you could ever imagine. Finding you, my dear, was not difficult."

"What…what are you going to do to me?" Sage stammered as she cowered against the tree branch.

"I *was* going to make you my apprentice," Josephine replied, "but you've lost that chance. You really shouldn't have run away from me."

"No!" Sage screamed as Josephine raised her hands and began to chant strange words. "Please stop," she begged one last time before everything went dark.

Sage's eyelids fluttered open. She felt dazed and confused as she looked at her surroundings. The air felt heavy and everything seemed distorted.

I'm in some sort of glass jar, Sage realized.

Suddenly, everything began to shake.

"Hello, Sage," Josephine called down.

Sage screamed and covered her ears. Josephine's voice was so loud and her body was so big.

Wait a minute, Sage gasped, looking around herself. *Josephine isn't big – I'm tiny!*

"That's right," Josephine confirmed, reading Sage's thoughts. "You're doomed to live in a glass jar forever. Don't worry about being lonely though. I have many friends for you. I'll even display this jar on the main shelf in my lair – it'll look wonderful!"

Sage watched in horror as Josephine began to throw miniature people into the jar. She kept tossing them in until there was no room to move.

"No!" Sage screamed as she felt herself being crushed by people in flowing dresses and heavy jewelry. "Let me out! I'll be your apprentice! Please, anything but this!"

"You possess magic," Josephine replied. "Just use your powers to transport yourself out of there."

"I can't!" Sage yelled. "I don't know how!"

"That's too bad," Josephine said with an evil smile. "Self-transportation was the first spell I was going to teach you!"

* * *

Home Grown Flowers

"We've got quite an addition to our class," Mrs. Waybourne said in a friendly, yet slightly confused tone.

Sixteen-year-old Bridget Rye looked up to see four girls standing at the front of the classroom with Mrs. Waybourne.

"I wonder why the principal is putting so many students in our class," Lauren Weller, Bridget's best friend, whispered. "It's weird."

Bridget nodded as she continued to stare at the girls. She found them to be odd and almost creepy, but she couldn't figure out why she felt that way.

"This is Holly, Poppy, Jasmine and Primrose Walker," Mrs. Waybourne introduced the sisters. "They've just transferred from..." she paused briefly. "What school did you say you were from?"

"We didn't," Primrose, the smallest of the four sisters, said.

Holly, the tallest sister, shot Primrose a warning glance and then smiled at Mrs. Waybourne. "Where should we sit?" she asked, changing the topic quickly.

"We'll need to make seating arrangements," Mrs. Waybourne replied, obviously unprepared for the new students. "Bridget, Lauren, would you mind taking the Walkers to the janitor's office? Tell him we need four more desks and chairs."

"Yes, Mrs. Waybourne," Lauren said as she stood up obediently.

Bridget suppressed the urge to roll her eyes. Lauren, the most polite student in the school, was always chosen to do tasks for teachers. Since Bridget was always with Lauren, she was called upon when the chore required two people.

Bridget stood up with less enthusiasm than Lauren and walked towards the door. She stopped suddenly when she heard the class burst into laughter.

Are they laughing at me? Bridget wondered as she turned around. She was relieved to see that no one was paying attention to her.

"That's so gross!" a girl, who sat at the front of the classroom, shrieked.

"Poppy soiled her panties!" another boy choked out. He was laughing so hard that tears flowed down his face.

"What are they talking about?" Poppy asked her sisters in confusion.

Jasmine cleared her throat and then pointed directly at the mess on the floor.

"I didn't!" Poppy protested, finally understanding the situation.

Bridget followed the horrified gazes of her classmates. There, right where Poppy was standing, was a pile of brown mush.

"What in the world?" Bridget exclaimed in shock. "I'll show you the way to the bathroom," she hurried to offer.

Bridget hadn't intended to embarrass Poppy even more with her comment, but it appeared as if she had.

"I didn't soil myself!" Poppy protested. Her face was now a dark shade of pink. "It's just mud!"

Poppy's claim only made the already hysterical boy laugh harder. His laughter was contagious, encouraging the other boys in the class to join in. Most of the girls looked on in disgust; even Lauren looked like she was about to be ill.

"That is enough, class!" Mrs. Waybourne scolded. However, she also looked paler than usual.

"I think we should get the chairs and desks now," Lauren commented, trying to save Poppy's feelings.

"Tell the janitor that we need a mop and perhaps a change of pants for Poppy," Mrs. Waybourne instructed as Bridget, Lauren and the Walkers began to leave the classroom.

"It really is mud," Holly said once they were in the hallway. "Show them your shoes, Poppy."

Poppy obediently lifted her left foot and then her right. Both of her sneakers were covered in mud.

"It's just mud," Bridget realized with relief.

"Of course," Holly said while rolling her eyes. "She must've stepped in mud before coming to school."

"Just mud," Lauren repeated to herself, feeling a lot better now.

"We've established that," Holly snapped.

Bridget didn't like Holly's attitude, but she bit her tongue and decided to give her the benefit of the doubt. After all, they were new and would still be adjusting to the school.

"Let's just get our desks and chairs," Jasmine said, before walking straight towards the janitor's office.

"How do you know where the janitor's office is?" Bridget asked in surprise, while trying to keep up with Jasmine. "Have you been there before?"

"Never, but I guess you could say I have an instinct that tells me where to go," Jasmine replied mysteriously.

Bridget was confused by Jasmine's comment, but she was even more confused when she saw Holly give Jasmine a warning glance.

"Can we just go to the janitor's office?" Primrose whined like a four-year-old.

"Stop whining," Holly scolded, as if Primrose's behavior was completely normal for an eleventh grader. "There's no rush. The janitor won't be there for another ten minutes – he's running late."

"How do you know that?" Bridget inquired suspiciously.

"I just do," Holly replied.

When the six girls reached the janitor's office, Bridget was shocked to discover that the janitor was indeed ten minutes late. *What's going on here?* she wondered in bewilderment.

Bridget was still thinking about the Walker sisters, especially Holly and Jasmine, later that day. There was something about them that didn't seem normal.

"We should go to the gym before the bell rings or we'll have to wait in line for the change-rooms," Lauren said, putting her empty lunch container into her backpack.

Lauren's voice brought Bridget back to reality. She'd been so engrossed in her thoughts that she had forgotten Lauren was beside her.

"Alright," Bridget replied.

In silence, the two friends walked towards the gym.

I wonder if Lauren's thinking about the Walker sisters too, Bridget contemplated.

After quickly changing into shorts and t-shirts, Bridget and Lauren headed towards the main part of the gym.

"We'll have the whole gym to ourselves for at least five minutes," Lauren commented, just before opening the doors. "Do you want to play some one-on-one basketball?"

Bridget never answered Lauren because she was too busy staring at Holly, Poppy, Jasmine and Primrose. The Walker sisters all wore t-shirts and shorts, revealing skin which was a ghastly shade of green.

"Oh my gosh!" Lauren exclaimed, finally noticing the odd sight.

"Hi!" Primrose replied excitedly in a voice that sounded as if it belonged to a six-year-old.

"Your skin..." Bridget choked out.

"What about it?" Poppy asked in confusion.

"It's so green!" Lauren cried, while looking at the girls' arms and legs.

"You're so mean," Primrose said with a whimper, right before tears began rolling down her face.

"Why are you crying?" Poppy asked Primrose, while wearing a blank expression on her face.

"She's crying because Bridget and Lauren are making fun of our skin color," Holly said in a matter-of-fact tone. "I told you we should've worn long-sleeved tops and sweat pants."

"We're not making fun of you," Bridget protested truthfully. "Please don't cry," she added to Primrose. "It's just that your skin doesn't look normal. Are you sick or something?"

"No," Jasmine replied bluntly. "We just went swimming in a polluted lake, that's all."

"You went swimming in a polluted lake?" Lauren cried. "But that's so dangerous! You might be really sick!"

"We're *not* sick," Jasmine snapped. "Now leave us alone."

Shocked, Bridget and Lauren watched as the four sisters walked to the other side of the gym.

"Something's definitely not right here," Bridget muttered.

"You can say that again," Lauren replied shakily. "How do you explain swimming in a lake at this time of year? The water would be zero degrees – at best!"

"Their faces look healthy," Bridget added quickly. She remembered that the first thing she'd noticed about the Walker sisters were their brightly colored faces.

Bridget and Lauren didn't have a chance to talk any longer as their classmates entered the gym. Laughter and gasps sounded when everyone saw the Walker sisters. This only made Primrose cry harder. After the gym teacher calmed Primrose down, he inquired about the color of their skin. Holly said it was caused by a science experiment accident in their old school. The gym teacher said no more on the matter after all the sisters claimed they were in good health.

"Jasmine said they were green because they swam in a polluted lake," Bridget whispered to Lauren. "Either Jasmine or Holly is lying."

"Yes, but which one?" Lauren whispered back.

"Probably both. I don't trust either of them."

Bridget was so tired after her unusual day at school that all she wanted to do was go home and curl up in front of the television. However, she'd signed up for the archery club which started today at 4 PM.

Bridget didn't have a lot of school spirit and usually wouldn't join after-school activities. Unfortunately the decision wasn't hers to make, when Mrs. Waybourne told Mrs. Rye that Bridget needed to be more involved in school activities. Her mother, who had high hopes of her daughter attending a prestigious university, promised that Bridget would join a club. Initially, Bridget refused, but after being lectured for hours she finally gave in and agreed to join the archery club.

Bridget sighed as she headed towards the gym for the second time that day. However, she sighed even louder when she saw who was already in the gym.

"Hello," Jasmine greeted in an unfriendly tone.

"Hey," Bridget replied, slightly concerned by the way Jasmine held the bow and arrow.

Holding the bow in her left hand, Jasmine used her right hand to casually toss the arrow in the air and catch it. She smiled smugly the whole time, as if this precision was effortless.

"You better watch you don't hurt yourself," Bridget advised.

"Oh, I won't hurt *myself*," Jasmine promised with a sly smile.

Bridget backed up as Jasmine proceeded towards her with the arrow pointed forward.

I wish the others would hurry up and get here, Bridget thought, realizing for the first time that she and Jasmine were alone in the soundproof gym.

"You look a little worried," Jasmine said with false concern. "Is everything okay?"

Bridget gulped hard as Jasmine brought the sharp silver tip of the arrow closer to her chest. "What...what are you doing?" she stuttered.

"What do you mean?" Jasmine mocked, pointing the arrow even closer to her.

Don't just stand there – do something! Bridget's instincts seemed to yell at her.

Reacting on impulse, Bridget grabbed the wooden base of the arrow Jasmine was holding and attempted to throw it away. She instantly regretted her decision as she saw the arrow pierce Jasmine's sickly green arm. Bridget couldn't believe her eyes as a gooey white liquid seeped out of Jasmine's arm.

"What's wrong with you?" Bridget cried in horror.

"What's wrong with me?" Jasmine seethed as she pressed the edge of her t-shirt against her cut arm. "The question should be what's wrong with you."

"You were going to attack me!" Bridget exclaimed.

"No, I wasn't. I was just trying to scare you."

"How was I supposed to know that you were just joking?" Bridget asked quietly, more to herself than to Jasmine.

Bridget looked at the arrow which was now lying on the floor. It was just a piece of wood and metal now, but seconds ago it was a deadly weapon. She looked up from the floor as she heard the coach and students arriving.

As Jasmine picked up the arrow, Bridget immediately noticed that the cut on her arm had magically stopped seeping the white goo.

"Just leave me and my sisters alone," Jasmine hissed, before joining the others.

Bridget was so shaken-up by the incident that she could hardly hold the bow and arrow steady. On her first attempt to fire the arrow, it dropped in front of her feet, and on the second try, it didn't go much further.

"Try to hold your hand steady," the coach instructed Bridget.

Bridget tried to do what her coach said, but it was no use; she just couldn't keep her hands from shaking.

"Why don't you let someone else have a turn?" the coach said with a smile, while taking the bow and arrow from Bridget and handing it to Jasmine. "Don't be nervous," the coach whispered to Bridget. "We're all rooting for you."

Bridget knew that the coach was wrong; Jasmine was certainly not rooting for her.

"Have you ever shot a bow and arrow before?" the coach asked Jasmine.

"No," she confessed.

"First you place your hand here and raise the bow to..." the coach began to instruct Jasmine.

"I don't need any help," Jasmine interrupted.

"But...but you said you've never used a bow and arrow before," the coach stuttered, obviously shocked by Jasmine's rudeness. "You need basic instructions."

"No, I don't," Jasmine replied cheekily as she placed the arrow against the bow and shot it towards the target board.

The arrow landed directly in the center of the target board, causing everyone to gasp.

"You were just joking about never using a bow and arrow before," the coach said in relief.

"No joke," Jasmine said sharply. "I've never touched a bow and arrow before today."

"That...that must've been beginner's luck then," the coach said, still stumbling with his words.

"Give me another arrow and you'll find out."

I can't believe the way Jasmine is talking to the coach! Bridget thought.

Everyone was quiet as Jasmine prepared to shoot again. It seemed as if everything happened in slow motion, from the time Jasmine released the arrow to the time it hit the end of the arrow that was already on the target board. No one said anything as they looked at the long arrow, which was really two arrows combined, sitting in the center of the board.

Jasmine snatched another arrow from the coach's hand and did the same thing again. Now there were three arrows attached to each other on the target board.

"That's incredible! That's unbelievable!" the coach cried. "I've never seen anything like it before!"

Neither have I, Bridget thought as she crept out of the gym. *But it's not incredible. It's downright scary.*

Bridget didn't say a word during dinner that night. Of course, her mother didn't notice.

Mrs. Rye was an accountant for the largest car dealership in their city. She took her job very seriously and often acted like she was at work even when she was at home. Bridget and her mother didn't have a close relationship, to say the least.

When Mrs. Rye's cellphone began to ring, Bridget had an epiphany. She would look in the new telephone book that had been delivered to their house just yesterday.

Surely the Walkers will be listed in it, Bridget reasoned.

Mrs. Rye had taken the telephone book into her den last night, and since Bridget wasn't allowed in there without permission, she waited for her mother to get off the phone. She tried to make eye contact with her and she even coughed loudly, but her mother wouldn't even acknowledge her. Bridget knew her mother would be on the phone for hours, so she left the table and crept quietly into her mother's den. She quickly found the telephone book and searched for the name Walker. She sighed as she saw about fifty people with that last name in her city.

Unhappy, Bridget left her mother's den and then grabbed her jacket. She needed some time to think, and she knew she'd get just that by taking a stroll around the block.

"I'm back from my walk!" Bridget called as she wiped her muddy shoes on the door mat. "That's if you even noticed I was gone," she added under her breath.

"Come into my den right now!" Mrs. Rye called back.

Bridget cringed as she suddenly remembered leaving the telephone book on her mother's desk. She tried to make herself look small and ashamed as she stood at the entrance to her mother's den.

"I presume this is your doing," Mrs. Rye said with a serious expression as she pointed to the telephone book on her desk.

"Yes," Bridget replied quietly.

Mrs. Rye sighed when she saw the pitiful look on her daughter's face. "You should've asked me if you wanted to use something from my den. You know my office is off-limits. I'm not angry that you used the telephone book, but I am angry that you defied my orders."

I defied your orders? Bridget thought in bewilderment. *I'm your daughter – not your employee.* She felt her blood boil. "I apologize," she said through clenched teeth.

"Your apology is accepted," Mrs. Rye replied in a serious tone. "However, you will have to be disciplined. I think an appropriate punishment would be for you to clean and organize the library."

"Yes, Mother," Bridget replied spitefully.

As Bridget started to leave, she thought about how different she was from her mother. Bridget had an inquisitive mind and didn't take herself too seriously. Mrs. Rye, on the other hand, was very strict and always had a professional demeanor. She often referred to the family's small room, which was filled with about five hundred books, as a library. However, in this case, Bridget didn't care about her mother's exaggeration; she was just glad she didn't have to clean a real library.

"Bridget," Mrs. Rye said sternly.

Bridget turned around to see her mother pointing to the telephone book which still lay on her desk.

"Sorry," Bridget said as she put the telephone book back in its original place. *That book has caused a lot of trouble and it didn't even give me information about the Walkers,* she thought in frustration.

Deciding to get the task over with, Bridget sighed deeply as she opened the door to the library. As she stepped inside, darkness surrounded her. She swept her fingers over the wall until she found the light switch. As she waited for her eyes to adjust to the sudden change in light, she tried to remember the last time she'd been in this room – it must have been at least six months.

When Bridget's eyesight returned to normal, she realized that the room was already neat, with the exception of a few books that lay on a chair and side table. It appeared that her main task would be dusting.

Bridget let out a loud sneeze as she dusted the bookshelf. Her nose itched and her throat felt dry. Before continuing to dust, she pulled the neck of her shirt protectively over her face, leaving only her eyes exposed. All the while, she cursed her mother for making her do this.

After the room was dust-free, Bridget began placing the scattered books back on the bookshelf. She grumbled as she picked up a long thin book that was titled, *Victorian Age: The Meaning of Flowers.*

"I'm so sick of flowers," Bridget said aloud, while thinking about how the Walker sisters were all named after flowers.

Bridget was about to put the book on the shelf when curiosity got the better of her. She suddenly had an urge to see what the book said about the holly, poppy, jasmine and primrose flowers.

Flipping to the index, Bridget ran her finger over the "J" section until she found jasmine. She quickly turned to page forty-eight and saw a beautiful picture of a white and pink flower.

"Jasmine," Bridget began reading out loud, "represents preciseness. Originally found in..." she suddenly stopped reading as images of the day's events flashed in her mind. She remembered Jasmine's comment about her innate ability to know where things were, such as the extra desks and chairs. Even creepier was how she'd shot three arrows with exact precision. It was as if Jasmine was born with the ability of accuracy.

Not wanting to believe such an absurd thing, Bridget quickly looked up the holly flower.

"Holly represents foresight," Bridget read while remembering Holly's prediction about the janitor's tardiness. "Holly foretold what was going to happen," she muttered with fear.

Shakily, Bridget turned to the page dedicated to poppies.

"Poppies represent oblivion," Bridget whispered with a shiver, all the while picturing Poppy standing in confusion as she continually asked what was going on. "Poppy really is oblivious."

Bridget's fingers flew over the pages until her eyes settled on an image of small yellow flowers. "The primrose," she read slowly, "represents early youth." Bridget felt like fainting as she recalled how Primrose whined and cried like a baby.

Bridget looked up from the book. Her body felt cold and tingled with fear. She didn't even react to the thump that the book made when it fell from her hands and onto the floor.

"They're flowers," Bridget was hardly able to choke out. "The Walker sisters are flowers."

Bridget had trouble sleeping that night. She tossed and turned for hours until falling into a restless sleep at 3 AM.

She dreamt that she was walking peacefully around beautiful beds of colorful flowers on a warm summer's day. Suddenly, clouds darkened the area, causing Bridget to have an overwhelming feeling that something was wrong. She began running towards the only exit gate which was located behind large flower beds filled with dark purple, dark blue and black flowers. As Bridget ran, the dark colored flowers began growing at an alarming rate. Their stems turned into a ghastly shade of green and slithered towards her. She was so close to the exit – just a few more feet and she would be free. Bridget screamed as a stem wrapped around her ankle and pulled her down. She hit the ground with a hard thud and then her body went numb as the stem squeezed her to death.

Bridget's eyes flung open. Her heart raced and sweat drenched her body. *It was just a dream*, she told herself.

Bridget smiled, knowing that she was safe from the deadly flowers in her dream. However, one glance at her backpack on the floor reminded her of the reason she had dreamt about killer flowers in the first place. Numbly, she sat up in bed.

"It's a living nightmare," Bridget muttered, wholly giving up on the idea of getting any peaceful slumber.

"You look awful!" Lauren exclaimed as Bridget walked down the school hallway later that morning.

"Then I look how I feel," Bridget muttered.

Bridget had only known the Walker sisters for twenty-four hours, but in that little time they had turned her life upside down. All during breakfast, she had contemplated telling Lauren about her startling discovery. However, after arriving at school, she suddenly changed her mind and decided to say nothing. Bridget was sure that Lauren would think she was either lying or absolutely crazy.

"Don't you feel well?" Lauren asked with a pout.

"Obviously not," Bridget snapped. "Leave me alone."

Bridget immediately regretted her harsh words when she saw the hurt expression on Lauren's face.

"Fine, I'll back off," Lauren said, giving Bridget a confused glance before walking away.

Bridget sighed. The day hadn't started off well and she knew it would only get worse unless she did something about the Walkers.

All throughout the morning, Bridget watched the Walker sisters closely. As she noted their unusual behavior and appearance, a plan slowly formed in her mind. By the time lunch arrived, Bridget was nervous but determined to get rid of the Walkers once and for all.

As the other students walked towards the lunchroom, Bridget hurried in the opposite direction. She'd finally reached the science lab, but as she carefully peeked inside, she was disappointed to see a teacher talking to a student. Nevertheless, Bridget ducked down, hurried into the classroom and hid behind a large desk.

"I have to tell the principal what you've done," the science teacher said.

Is he talking to me? Bridget thought in horror.

"I said I was sorry," a boy, who was talking to the teacher, protested. "I didn't mean to cut Amanda's hair – really, I didn't!"

He hasn't spotted me, Bridget realized thankfully.

"My decision is final," the science teacher said firmly.

Bridget backed up against the desk and watched tensely as they left the room. Not wasting a second, she sprang into action and opened the cabinet that contained chemicals. She grabbed the spray bottle marked, "Plant Poison" and then hurried out of the science room.

I'm glad I paid attention to the horticulture unit in science class, Bridget thought proudly while clutching the spray bottle.

Heather Beck

After entering the lunchroom, Bridget searched for the Walker sisters. Her heart sank as she realized they weren't there. Suddenly, out of the corner of her eye, Bridget saw a sad-looking Lauren sitting near the doors that led outside.

I bet the Walkers are outside, Bridget thought as she ran past Lauren.

"Hey!" Lauren shouted in surprise.

Instead of acknowledging her friend, Bridget bolted out the door.

It was sunny outside and a cool wind blew against Bridget's face. She squinted but, almost immediately, she spotted four girls sitting on a bench.

Bridget's heart raced when she realized she'd finally found the Walker sisters. Keeping a tight grip on the bottle of plant poison, she marched towards the girls.

Of course it's them, Bridget sneered. *No normal person would eat outside on a day like this.* Her skin crawled while imagining what Holly, Poppy, Jasmine and Primrose ate for lunch.

"Hi, Bridget!" Primrose called in a tone that sounded like it belonged to a little girl. "Hi, Lauren!" she added quickly.

"Go back to the lunchroom!" Bridget snapped after turning around to face Lauren.

"No!" Lauren shot back. "I'm not leaving until you tell me what's going on with you."

"Leave," Bridget pleaded. "It's for your own good."

"You're really starting to scare me," Lauren said in a slightly shaky voice.

"I'm scared too," Holly said suddenly. "Tell me what you're hiding behind your back, Bridget. I can't foresee your actions because your mind is so mud-

111

dled. Even you don't know what you're going to do next."

"Yes, I do!" Bridget cried, revealing the spray bottle of plant poison and thrusting it towards the Walker sisters.

"What's that?" Poppy asked in confusion.

"You really live up to your name, Poppy," Bridget said, feeling fully in control. "So do your sisters."

"What's going on?" Lauren demanded.

"Tell me," Bridget continued while ignoring her friend. "How were you created? How do you turn a flower into a person?"

"Bridget, you're crazy!" Lauren cried.

"I'm not crazy – whoever invented the Walker sisters is the crazy one," Bridget said passionately, while glancing at Lauren for a moment. "They're flowers. They're walking, talking flowers."

"They're just regular teenagers," Lauren pleaded with Bridget.

"Bridget's completely right about us being flowers," Jasmine interrupted calmly. "However, she's wrong about our maker, Mrs. Walker. She isn't crazy – she doesn't even know what's happened."

"What did happen?" Bridget demanded while still pointing the spray bottle towards the sisters.

"You humans know nothing," Jasmine laughed bitterly. "You have no clue you're being watched by every flower and tree. We're all alive and experience the same emotions as humans." The smirk on Jasmine's face faded quickly. "Actually, we don't have the same feelings as humans – we're better than humans and can feel more joy and pain than you could ever imagine. We, the flowers and the trees, are superior to humans in every aspect but one – we can't walk."

"You're walking now," Bridget observed in disgust.

"I guess humans are smarter than we give them credit for," Jasmine mocked.

"You're meant to stand for precision, not cruelty," Bridget pointed out harshly.

"Cruelty?" Jasmine shrieked. "Don't you dare talk to me about cruelty! Humans are the cruelest creatures on the planet. You stand on us. You cut our stems and put us in vases. You even cut our heads off and then press them in books!"

"Humans are horrible to plants – I get it!" Bridget cried with impatience. "But that doesn't explain how you've transformed into a human!"

"I don't have to tell you anything," Jasmine seethed. "I owe you nothing."

"Stop it!" Holly yelled. "I can see how this will end and it's not pretty. I'll tell you how we grew our bodies, if you put that bottle down."

Curiosity got the better of Bridget as she slowly lowered the spray bottle.

"Just keep it down," Holly warned. "That plant poison could kill us."

"That was the plan," Bridget said with a tight smile.

"We don't have to tell them anything," Jasmine repeated angrily.

"Yes, we do," Holly said knowingly, before taking a deep breath and looking at Bridget and Lauren with intense eyes. "Mrs. Walker grew Poppy, Jasmine, Primrose and myself from seed and cared for us with the utmost love. She lavished us with plant food and sprinkled us with water each day. Then one day, after we'd blossomed into beautiful flowers, Mrs. Walker cut herself on a sharp blade of grass that grew nearby. Drops of blood landed on Poppy,

Jasmine, Primrose and I, and the next thing we knew, we had grown into humans. The love of the woman who cultivated us gave us life."

"Is...is this for real?" Lauren asked in a shaky voice.

"Yes," Holly replied.

"It's not normal!" Bridget cried out suddenly, lifting the spray bottle up once again.

"Don't hurt us," Primrose pleaded. "Just leave us alone."

"There's no point in begging," Jasmine said, putting an arm protectively around Primrose's shoulders. "Humans aren't reasonable creatures."

"You're flowers masquerading as humans. Do you really think I can just look the other way?" Bridget cried in frustration.

"Yes," Holly replied calmly. "Yes, you can."

"I...I can't," Bridget stuttered.

"You have to," Lauren said, almost in tears.

Bridget's eyes fell upon the Walker sisters. She saw the familiar look of anger on Jasmine's face, but this time she realized the cause of her anger. Jasmine had seen terrible things happen to flowers; she felt as if she could never trust a human. No longer wanting to see the pain that Jasmine harbored, Bridget turned her eyes towards Poppy. She almost laughed when she saw the confused, yet innocent expression on her beautiful face. Bridget's eyes then traveled to Primrose. Realizing that she was just a child, Bridget suddenly felt terrible for causing her so much fear. Next, Bridget's eyes turned to Holly, who looked very happy and grateful. It only took Bridget a second to realize why Holly, the one blessed with the power of foresight, was smiling.

Holly knows what's going to happen, Bridget realized before she dropped the spray bottle harmlessly on the ground.

Primrose smiled widely as she hugged Bridget. "Thank you," she whispered.

"I'm so sorry," Bridget whispered back.

* * *

The three remaining months in the school year passed quickly as Bridget spent them getting to know Holly, Poppy, Jasmine and Primrose. Bridget was extremely surprised with Jasmine's change of attitude. Although Jasmine still claimed to hate some humans, she admitted to being quite fond of Lauren and even Bridget.

Bridget, Lauren and their four new friends were inseparable during the summer. They spent their days playing games, telling stories, swimming in Lauren's pool and window shopping at the mall. As the summer came to an end, Bridget noticed a change in the Walker sisters' behavior. However, Lauren didn't seem to notice any difference. Instead, she continued to talk excitedly about the upcoming school year.

"Hurry up," Lauren begged Bridget as they walked to school on a cool September morning. "I promised the Walkers that we'd meet them in their garden by 8:30, and it's already 8:37!"

Bridget obediently followed Lauren, but she did so with a heavy heart. She felt as if something wasn't right.

"Holly! Poppy! Jasmine! Primrose!" Lauren called after she and Bridget entered the Walker sisters' garden. "Where are they?" she asked in confusion.

Before Bridget had a chance to reply, an old woman came out of a nearby house.

"You two frightened me!" the plump woman with graying hair exclaimed.

"I'm sorry," Lauren apologized. "We were just looking for our friends."

Bridget shot Lauren a warning glance. The last thing they needed was for this woman to ask why they were looking for their friends in a garden.

"I haven't seen anyone here," the woman replied before bending down to sprinkle plant food over some flowers. "Oh, no!" she exclaimed suddenly.

"What's wrong?" Bridget asked with a pounding heart.

"Oh, no!" the old woman repeated. "I've been looking for my favorite collection of flowers since last spring. I thought they had grown legs and walked off," she chuckled at the thought. "But now I've found them and they're dead." The old woman pushed aside healthy flowers to reveal a holly, poppy, jasmine and primrose flower lying shriveled in the dirt.

"No!" Lauren cried upon seeing the state of her friends.

"I agree that the loss of a flower is unfortunate, but it's not like they were people," the old woman said before casting Lauren an odd look and then walking back to her house.

"That wasn't Mrs. Walker, was it?" Lauren asked, still obviously shaken up.

"I suppose it was," Bridget replied sadly.

"Well, she didn't look very concerned about her flowers!" Lauren cried.

"She hasn't truly experienced the power of flowers," Bridget explained, "but we have."

"Do you think Holly, Poppy, Jasmine and Primrose will come alive next spring?" Lauren asked, while trying to hold back her tears.

"I guess we'll just have to wait and see," Bridget replied as she stared at a long, sharp blade of grass.

* * *

About the Author

Heather Beck is a Canadian author and screen-writer who began writing professionally at the age of sixteen. Her first book was published when she was only nineteen years old. Since then she has written several well-reviewed books.

Heather recently received an Honors Bachelor of Arts from university where she specialized in English and studied an array of disciplines. Currently, she is working on two young adult novels and has five anthologies slated for publication. As a screenwriter, Heather has multiple television shows and movies in development. Her short films include *Young Eyes*, *The Rarity* and *Too Sensible For Love*.

Besides writing, Heather's greatest passion is the outdoors. She is an award-winning fisherwoman and a regular hiker. Her hobbies include swimming, playing badminton and volunteering with non-profit organizations.